THIS CENSUS-TAKER

By China Miéville

King Rat

Perdido Street Station

The Scar

Iron Council

Looking for Jake & Other Stories

Un Lun Dun

The City & The City

Kraken

Embassytown

Railsea

Three Moments of an Explosion: Stories

The Last Days of New Paris

China Miéville

THIS CENSUS-TAKER

A Novella

PICADOR

First published 2016 by Picador

This edition published in paperback 2017 by Picador
an imprint of Pan Macmillan
20 New Wharf Road, London N1 9RR
Associated companies throughout the world
www.panmacmillan.com

ISBN 978-1-5098-1213-4

1 3 5 7 9 8 6 4 2

A CIP catalogue record for this book is available from the British Library.

Printed and bound by CPI Group (UK) Ltd, Croydon, CR0 4YY

To Mic

For all their help with this book, my deepest thanks to Mark Bould, Mic Cheetham, Julie Crisp, Rupa DasGupta, Maria Dahvana Headley, Simon Kavanagh, Tessa McWatt, Susie Nicklin, Sue Powell, Max Schaefer, and Rosie Warren. I'm very grateful to all at Macmillan and Picador, especially Nicholas Blake, Robert Clark, Ansa Khan Khattak, Neil Lang, Ravi Mirchandani, and Lauren Welch; and all at Random House, in particular Keith Clayton, Penelope Haynes, David Moench, Tricia Narwani, Scott Shannon, David G. Stevenson, Annette Szlachta-McGinn, my editor Mark Tavani, and Betsy Wilson.

Much of this book was written during a fellowship at the MacDowell Colony, Peterborough, NH; and then as a residency fellow of the Lannan Foundation, in Marfa, TX. I am profoundly grateful to both organizations for their generous support.

Among the countless writers to whom I'm indebted, I want here to pay particular tribute to Mary Butts, Barbara Comyns, Jane Gaskell, John Hawkes, Denis Johnson, Anna Kavan, Edward St Aubyn, and Roland Topor.

'Like all these long low squat houses, it had been built not *for* but *against*. They were built against the forest, against the sea, against the elements, against the world. They had roof-beams and doors and hatred – as though in this part of the world an architect always included hatred among his tools, and said to his apprentice: "Mind you've brought along enough hatred today."'

Jane Gaskell, Some Summer Lands

THIS CENSUS-TAKER

A boy ran down a hill path screaming. The boy was I. He held his hands up and out in front of him as if he'd dipped them in paint and was coming to make a picture, to press them down to paper, but all there was on him was dirt. There was no blood on his palms.

He was nine years old, I think, and this was the fastest he'd ever run, and he stumbled and careered and it seemed many times as if he would fall into the rocks and gorse that surrounded the footpath, but I kept my feet and descended into the shadow of my hill. The air felt wet but no rain had fallen. I sent up cold dust behind me and little animals scuttling ahead.

People in the town saw that cloud long before I arrived, Samma would later tell me. When she was sure that it wasn't just weather, she was one of those who came to wait by the pump beyond the bridge to the west, where there were the last buildings, to watch whatever was coming. After that day, when I saw her, when she could, Samma would tell me stories, including the story of when I came down the hill.

'I knew it was you,' she'd say. 'That dirt devil on its way down. "It's the boy," I said. A lot of us did. You must've run a mile while I watched you, you ran and ran and you didn't slow once. You came right past the nails.' The nails: my name that she had adopted for a copse of dead white bushes. 'Right by every split in the hill, and you must have heard all the devils down there howling at you.' When she talked like this I'd stare at her urgently, without speaking. 'We heard you coming, making noises like a hurt gull or something, and I said: "It is, it's the boy!"'

In I'd come. I turned with the path, away from where the slope grew drier and stonier and inclined precipitously, and I ran for where the crowd was waiting. I could see down spaces between those outmost walls to the town's built-up bridge. I was weeping so hard I retched, came loud and filthy past the wire-spinning mill and the glassworks, past barns and stores and the ground before them strewn with old straw and the shards of things that had been broken within, toward the cobbles and concrete in view of that bridge itself, where the townspeople waited.

There were children among them: those with adults were held back by them. I made noises as if I were a whooping baby. I struggled for air.

I was the only one moving while all there stared at my little figure raising dirt, until someone, I don't know who, started forward to meet me, and they brought others after them in shame, Samma among them.

They ran to me with their own arms out like mine, to take me.

'Look!' I heard a man say. 'God, look at him!'

I kept up the hands I thought were bloody for them to see.

I shouted, 'My mother killed my father!'

—

I was an uphiller. Above my house was a steepening distance of grass and loose earth, then slabs of flint in a rough ziggurat, and then at last, out of sight, the peak. No path went there. We lived as high on the hill as anyone. Our house was at the same level of the slope as those of a few weather-watchers and hermits and witches you could call our neighbours, though you'd have to walk a while from where we lived to see any of their places, and we never visited them nor they us.

My house had three storeys that grew less and less finished as they rose, as if the builders had lost spirit the further they were from the soil. On the ground were a kitchen with a parlour, my father's workroom, a passage and a cornering wooden stair. In the middle, two small, less finely finished bedrooms, my father's and my mother's, and a cubby where I slept between them.

On the highest floor any drive to subdivide had been defeated and there was only one space, into which you could feel air come through the imperfect outer walls and the cracks where window-frames met plaster.

I liked to climb the steep stairs to play alone in that wind-filled room. All the rest of the house was whitewashed or painted in an ochre made from local earth, but two walls of the attic were papered in a repeating design. The tangled flowers and pagodas astonished me. I couldn't imagine my mother or my father choosing them. I decided the paper must have predated my parents' arrival, which made me contemplate the house before they came to it, the house empty of them. That made me queasy and excited.

In the kitchen and where my father worked there were lights and tools that ran off current from the generator we would sometimes fire up. In the bedrooms we used candles.

The windows of the top floor had no curtains and every day the light would cross the room, from one end to the other. The wallpaper was faded by years of the sun's attention. In one corner, low down where I thought it would be secret, I drew animals around the buildings and among the stems.

My house stood by the path's end, wedged into the rocks of the hill as if shying back from where the ground fell away before it. Between the house and that drop was a rusted wire fence in front of which I'd stand to watch hill animals – feral and crossbred cats and dogs, dassies, the lean descendants of goat and sheep escapees – trip and scatter between stone shapes and the bushes. There were those beasts with territories I came to know, on which I came to know that I was encroaching, and those which visited repeatedly seemed curious about me – a furious drab songbird claiming certain trees, a red-furred dog not much bigger than a puppy but which moved with an older dog's caution.

From here I could make out the black roofs of the town. I'd kick stones small enough to go through the metal links and watch them bounce into the boscage, or further – all the way, I imagined, to the water, to the gulley below the buildings.

It was one town scattered up and down the sides of the two hills and between them on the bridge. And like everyone on both those hills, we were of it, though we lived in a house as far from the streets as it could be for that still to be true. It was the law of this town to which we were subject. When I came down that day, I wasn't running for the law, but the law found me.

The people comforted me in a rough way.

'What did you see, boy?' they asked. 'What happened?'

All I could do was cry.

'Your mum did something?' a woman said to me, kneeling and taking my shoulders in her hands. 'She did something to your dad? Tell us.'

She confused me. She was trying to make me meet her eye. What she said confused me because I didn't think she was describing what I'd seen, what I'd walked in on, but as she spoke I realized she was repeating what I'd told her. The boy, I, had said his mother killed his father.

Still now if I consider the thing I saw in my house that day what comes back to me first is my mother's hands: her calm expression, the sight of her braced and striking, her hands coming down hard, a knife, my father's eyes closed, a glimpse of his mouth, his mouth full of blood, blood on the pale flowers of the walls, and the boy has to think all that, first, I have no choice, I can't think around it, and every time it takes me a moment to reflect and prepare to say that no, that's not what it was, surely, that the face of the person being hit was hidden, or certainly that it wasn't my father's.

I tried to correct what I'd said that the woman was repeating, and could only swallow.

I'd heard a rhythm. I'd gone up to the top of the house, the space with all the air, and found people already there. By the bridge the woman looked at me and I concentrated, and I didn't think what I'd seen was my mother killing my father, as I'd said. I went back to it. Her face, my mother's face, blank and tired, yes, but if seen only for an instant, glimpsed. And not her hands coming down but my father's.

'No,' I said. 'My father. Someone. My mother.'

It had been my *father* with his back to me. I thought that as carefully as I could through all my shaking and gasping. Him holding someone. Her face I couldn't recall.

My father's back had been to me. It hadn't been my mother's back. That blood had been there, the blood I still imagined on my hands. I remember it as very bright and dark at the same time, because it was newly come into the light while the paper it coloured was so faded.

I'd screamed until my father turned to regard me. That was what I'd seen: him gasping from his efforts.

He stared at me and I ran away.

Some mornings my mother would give me lessons in letters and numbers. She didn't have many books but she'd place before me one of those she did and sit across the table from me and point without speaking at certain words, waiting as I struggled to say them. She would correct me when she had to and sometimes impatiently prompt me, sound out words at which I'd failed. This was in another language than the one in which I write now.

My mother was a muscular woman with dark grey skin folded on her forehead and around her eyes. Except when she was digging she left her long white-flecked hair loose so it draped around her face. I thought her beautiful but after she died if I ever heard anyone discuss her in more than brief passing the adjective they used was *strong* – or, once, *handsome*.

Mostly what my mother did was tend the sprawl of up-and-down land around our house. She'd separated this sloping garden into seemingly formless plots with boundaries she marked with stones. When she saw how they confused me, she told me she was following contour lines.

She would clear blown sticks and leaf-matter from between them, and dry it to feed our fire or the generator in its little housing for when we wanted electricity. She had an outside dress in which she kept seeds of different kinds. I'd sit quietly on one of several suitable stones and watch her reach into her many pockets to sow handfuls in the grit she tilled. Sometimes she smiled in a cold way at the anxiety her random methods raised in me.

Once she stood straight and leaned on her hoe and looked right at me and said, 'Last night I had a dream of planting bits of rubbish right here and watering them and making them grow. Growing a dump. When I say, "I had a dream" I mean I wanted to, not "It came into my head while I was sleeping."'

My mother would twist unpleasant figures out of wire and wood and put them up to frighten the birds. My father made them too, and his were finer than hers, but none of them intimidated the crows very much, and my mother and I would often have to run out of the house windmilling our arms and shouting so the big birds would lurch away from the seeds a while, less out of fear than a kind of languorous contempt.

Out of that thin dusty ground my mother pulled hybrids and rarities as well as beans and gourds and so on. Some of what she grew we ate; some she sold or bartered with the shopkeepers on the bridge or in the bridgetown, for all kinds of things. Some she exchanged for more seeds that she would fold back into the earth.

Mostly we kept to our own patch of hill, as did everyone who lived above the town: the path below us and all the ruts cutting crosswise from height to height ran carefully so as not to get too close to any dwellings. Yes, at rare times, almost, it felt in later years, out of some obligation to be naughty, a duty to something, I might walk a long while through complex country, creeping close enough to another uphiller's place below our own to see them from the shelter of bushes, to watch crooked women, sisters raising pigs in a barn, to see the gnarled man on his plateau out of sight of the second hill performing precise tasks in his yard, calibrating gauges on old machines the moving parts of which he would daub with grease. These other houses looked so much like my own that they roused in me imprecise suspicions, as if, I would later have the words to think, they were a set.

There was supposed to be a holy old woman or man living in a cave no more than an hour's walk from our door, just below the zenith, and I remember once glimpsing the beat of a brown cape like a shaken sheet, but whether that cloth was worn on bony vatic shoulders I can't say. I can't even say if I truly saw it.

I've observed real ascetics since, their mortifications and their dens, and I know now how pinchbeck was the self-exile I saw, if I saw anything, if there was anything to see.

The most common trace of those who lived closest to us was the smoke from their fires, from when they made food, or destroyed their rubbish, which was not how we disposed of ours.

My father was a very tall pale man who seemed endlessly startled, who moved in jerks as if trying not to be caught out. He made keys. His customers would come up from the town and ask for the things for which people usually ask – love, money, to open things, to know the future, to fix animals, to fix things, to be stronger, to hurt someone or save someone, to fly – and he'd make them a key.

I was put out of the house during these transactions but would often creep around the perimeter to crouch by the window of his workroom to hear the discussions, and even to peek in. More than once my mother, prodding at her plots, her hair up in the yellow scarf that was the brightest thing I ever saw her wear, observed me huddled by the sill. She never stopped me eavesdropping.

My father would take notes as people falteringly told him their needs. On rough brown paper he would start to sketch the outlines of a key's tines and troughs in graphite and ink, correcting the lines as his customers spoke. He'd continue when the visitors had left, sometimes drawing for hours, almost always finishing his rendition in a single sitting, even if it meant he was working until sun-up.

The next day he'd go and start our generator droning, and, returning, would pin the finished image by his table, pinch slats of metal in his vice and with minute movements and slow care, stopping frequently to refer to the picture, cut them with a screaming electric blade run for a few seconds at a time, dimming the downstairs lights, or by hand with the taut steel-wire saws I was also forbidden to touch. My father was strong despite his scrawny arms. He cut and shaped.

Behind his workbench he kept glass jars containing handfuls of various dusts. A few were deep colours; most were varieties of brown and dirt grey. He'd dip his fingers in one at a time, rub the emerging keys, polishing them with the powders and with the sweat on his thumb. I never saw him replenish any containers: he only ever used a trace.

The work exhausted him, even more than you might think. When he finished he'd hold up what he'd made and blow it clean and eye it thoughtfully, the key shining, he a dirty mess.

Sometimes days later those who'd commissioned him would come back to take what they must have paid for, though often not in the tin and paper money of the town, of which there was rarely much in our house; sometimes he would descend to bring the key to them. I never saw any customer more than once.

When my mother cooked mostly she did not talk, planning her garden, I think, neither meeting nor avoiding my eye. When he made supper, my father would step around the little kitchen and pass me food, smiling like a man trying to remember how to do it. He'd look eagerly at my mother and me, and she would not look back, and I would, though also without a word, and he'd try to ask us things and tell us stories.

—

'It's best to live up here,' my father told me. 'Where the air's good and thin, not too heavy. It doesn't get in the way.'

That's a brief memory. When he said that he and I were walking together down the path on an errand I don't remember. I hadn't realized it yet but I wasn't often alone in his company like that; my mother placed herself at the periphery of most of our interactions. I would go walking on my own, though, which she didn't stop, and so would he, and then I might see him, even follow him, though I tried not to let him see me.

On some days bigger and more intricate things than birds passed over us through that thin air, bustling and busy, too high for me to make them out. If I was in his sight when they did so, my father would try that smile again so I thought he wanted to explain something to me, but he never did.

I grew up with the constant wind of the hill whispering to me and pushing back my dark fringe. Behind its sounds were the faint and far-off and occasional shouts of animals and the clack of rock-fall. Sometimes there was an engine or the percussion of a distant shotgun.

I'd seen my father's furies before the day of that murder when his face and my mother's face flickered together. I call them furies but in those moments he was unmoved and unmoving: he looked as if he was distracted and thinking deeply.

When I was seven he killed a dog while I watched. It was not our dog. We didn't then keep any living thing.

I was upslope from my mother's garden in a splayed tree with roots tangling in the hill dirt. I remember the day as caustically bright, and I remember things overlooking me and gusting at the limits of the flat and open sky. So there I was:

the boy, stroked by leaves, not knowing where his mother was, watching his father.

The man sat smoking on an outcrop below. He was unaware of the boy's attention.

That small red dog came down from nowhere in particular in the heights. It had lived, I suppose, as after weaning all the semi-wild animals on the hill must, by stealing and begging, by luck, as well as by its hunting.

It came closer to my father with a hesitant hope-filled cringe. The man was motionless, his cigarette half-raised.

The dog came zig-zag closer, putting down careful steps between the pebbles. The man held out his hand and the animal stopped but he rubbed his finger and thumb together and the little dog sniffed and crept forward again. It licked his hand and he took it by the back of the neck. It struggled but not much: he knew how to hold a dog and it was not panicked.

He put his cigarette out on a stone. He examined that stone and rejected it and looked for a better one. A rush swept through the watching boy and made him shake. It was as if his own heartbeat punched him inside. His father searched.

I knew what he was going to do. This is the first memory I have of my father killing anything but I remember the certainty with which I watched him. It was strong enough that I wonder now if I've forgotten other, earlier such acts, that then I still remembered.

The man raised his chosen flint high and hit the dog with it. He brought it down on its head and it did not bark. He hit it again and again. The boy clung to the tree and watched and pushed one shaking hand into his mouth so as to be quiet like the dog. My fingers tasted of resin.

When he was done my father stood and looked into the

valley. It was a cold summer and everything was green; you couldn't see the river, the depths of the cut below the town and its bridge were so thick with trees. The dog dangled in my father's hand. He trudged up the slope.

Though I was full of terror, when he went from view behind a twist of landscape, I came down from the tree and went up too, staying hidden, waiting for him to emerge again into my sight. He didn't see me when he did. He ascended to the west and I crept after him behind rocks and undergrowth and in ditches. I followed him up the twisting way he took that wasn't a true path but that I could see he'd walked before. The dog's tail brushed the ground.

My father disturbed buzzards. They lifted off slowly and circled.

There was a cave mouth above and out of sight of our house and of the road. I had never before approached it from this direction and so was surprised at its appearance, but I knew it. I wasn't supposed to come here without my parents but sometimes I did.

When they took me, my mother and father would encourage me over its odd prim fringe of stone spurs that rose like a low fence at the threshold, and step over themselves into the shadow in the hill. They never came without a flashlight, and they would crank its handle and let its orange glow show their way on the tunnel floor. Even without that illumination, even when I came alone and was too afraid to go far, I could see the pit.

In their company I'd go forward slowly, tapping my way with a stick or my toes as if the rock floor was a trick, or crawling on all fours and patting the ground before each shuffle and slide as if the black split might ambush me.

This time I clung to a wind-carved stump and watched my father enter the hill. I came close enough to see. He was standing still and looking into our dump-hole.

The hole interrupted the passage, which continued beyond it into darkness. My father had shone his light across that gap for me so I'd seen the tunnel extend beyond the strength of the weak beam. The fissure was close to two metres wide.

Every three or four days, my whole life, my mother or my father hauled our sacks and boxes of rubbish here and tipped them into the hole. Holding me, my father would sometimes let me help, let me drop some in. You could hear the uncompostable refuse, the plastic wrappers weighted with stones or bones, the broken glass and what household junk we couldn't reuse, bounce and jostle against the sheer stone of the shaft and break apart and tumble into silence. You wouldn't hear it hit any bottom.

The vertical sides were always speckled with mould where what of our food waste my mother didn't give her garden smeared them on the way down. I would hold the rock of the cave walls while my mother or father disposed of all our trash, gripping and teasing myself with fear by pretending I might try to climb sideways over the gap, to continue into the hill.

My father stood at the lip. He looked down into the black for a long time then pulled back his arm and swung it forward and released the dead dog just so, so it arced up over the trash-pit hole and paused and accelerated down into it in a curve so perfect everything seemed to have led to it.

The dog was born to descend this way. Millions of years ago, the stone had split to receive it.

My father stared down into the hill with such focus it was as if he had done all of this, this killing, because he had to see an animal fall.

He might have seen me behind him on the way back but I don't think so. Certainly I tried very hard to keep out of his sight – though later I came to believe it likely wouldn't have mattered had I failed to. I followed him with my weak limbs shaking because I was even more afraid to be out there on the hill alone as the light went down, near the rubbish hole with the dead dog inside it, than to be behind him.

I didn't want to follow my father into the kitchen where he stood but it was cold and there was only one door into the house and we had no sheds or barns in which I might hide, and the concrete housing of the generator was tight, without space for me to slip into. There was only the outhouse, where I'd certainly be found. In the waning light I stopped at the garden's edge and stood like a tree. There I stared at my house, at the late sun filling the attic window, hearing only wind and my own breaths, until the evening drove me in to where my father and my mother waited.

I ran past them, holding my breath and not looking at them, up to the attic to hunker in my corner by the markings I'd made, to go exploring within them, keeping my gaze on them as the light diminished.

It was my father who came up at last to beckon me, to tell me it was time to eat. So I had to go back past him. I had to come down past him to where my mother sat at the table with her eyes half-closed and her head tilted back so she could look at me with a downward gaze no matter that I was standing. She watched me with a sullen coolness I now think was well-disguised concern.

It has no business being alive any more, but above me a cold-drunk wasp hovers about the chandelier's glowing ring. An escort of shadow wasps disperses and converges on the ceiling in perfect formation as the summer insect falls and imprecisely rises. One bulb is broken so the shadows don't surround the sluggish source-wasp but seem to flank it, to bring up its rear and suggest its way.

I can't bring myself to kill it.

When I came to this room I moved the table to the window so I could write as I do now, watching a city get dark and switch to neon. I'm an honoured guest here, which is why there are two guards outside my door to take care of me, for when I do my work. That's what my hosts said, with such courtesy and conviction that I wonder if they've come to believe it.

I've been working for many hours. I think those guards are probably lulled by the sounds in here. Which will continue.

There's still a smell of smoke. I'm biding my time. While it was light I wrote a tiny poll of the absent: four behind me (I wrote 'saw the sea; cut metal; stole a flouted order; twisted hooks on twine'), one perhaps also behind me, perhaps ahead – my predecessor. I burned the list.

This is my second book.

I started on my first book three years ago, in a distant country, and on my third book a year after that. Now at last it's time for me to start writing this second book.

The manager of my line told me, You never put anything down except to be read. Every word ever written is written to be read and if some go unread that's only chance, failure, they're like grubs that die without changing. He said, You'll keep three books.

So my first is a book of numbers. It's lists and calculations and, for efficiency, I write it using ciphers. There's a legend I never check any more, knowing all the signs now, the single-stroke shorthands that mean kilogram and tonne, widow, printer, generation, thief, the signs for currency, shipyard, doctor, for uncertainty, the holding sign that means there's an unknown factor here to which I'll come back. This first book's for everyone, though almost no one wants it or would know how to read it.

The third of my three books is for me. You'll keep one, is what he told me, for you alone to read, in which you should write secrets. But you'll never be sure that no one else *will* read them: that's the risk and that's how the third book works.

When he gave me that warning he held his finger up as if he was counting to one.

He said, You'll write it not because there's no possibility it'll be found but because it costs too much to *not* write it. If you ever find someone else's third book, it's up to you what you do. You could read it, but you don't have to. Nothing you'd read would be for you. If I found one, he said, what I'd do is I'd set fire to it. I wouldn't read it and I wouldn't give it to you.

If I got back someone's *second* book, well, I'd give you that, of course: the second book's for readers, he said. But you can't know when they'll come, if they do. It's the book for telling: no code for that one. But – he counted one again and had my close attention – you can still use it to tell secrets and send messages. Even so. You could say them right out, but you can hide them in the words, too; in their letters, in the ordering on lines, the arrangements and rhythms. He said, The second book's performance.

My third book is a notebook that fits in my hand. It's a quarter full already, with my smallest writing, using symbols for my secrets.

The first book is a ledger that we share, my manager and I, recording as per our job. Sometimes we slip loose leafs between its pages, with amendments, information we need.

My second book is this box of papers.

You can tell it any way you want, he said, you can be I or he or she or we or they or you and you won't be lying though you might be telling two stories at once. Inherit a second book from someone else, to continue it, and you can have a conversation with what's already there. Write on scraps and in its margins.

Yes, there are papers here from when this story was started, not by me.

Today we saw a big animal bigger than anything I ever seen, I read in the letters of someone very young, in this, my precocious precursor's first language, that I've come to know better than my own first, certainly in writing, in some part from these words she left me. She writes, *I am learning as we travel.*

There are other pieces: the impressions of a serious child; scattered scenes, any narrative impossible to reconstruct; snips of description, a few of which have stayed with me since I learned to read them, and to which I still repeatedly return –

There are raggedy people on the railway lines above; it has a snails eyes; in this country the water is thick.

Most of it was lost, my manager told me, before the remainder became mine. I've cross-referenced this book with the first, paged backward through the latter to find the statistics for what I think must be the town with thick water, or where there were people on lines overhead. I've wondered if we might return to any of those places, so I could double-check details and itemize them too, but that's just what we shouldn't need to do. Still there've been rare times when some feature where we stop has put me in mind of one of my predecessor's phrases – a flint cupola invoking a building *all cutty moonshaped grey*, stilted longhouses reminding me *dont fall theres things in the mud*. As if my boss retraces steps sometimes, absent-mindedly, or because tasks are unfinished, and we might one day come to the place with raised neglected rails where outcasts live.

Of the second book's early pages that I have, the last-but-one-written – you can tell from the more formal older hand – is notes toward a catechism. I know because it's labelled *Notes toward my catechism*.

It says *The Hope*, then that's crossed out, and what hope was this? After that is written *This Hate*, which is crossed out too. Then starting again the words congregate in curious and precise lines, with a child's care, for a reader to come:

The Hope Is So

the catechism says, and then,

Count Entire Nation. Subsume Under Sets -

Below that there's a mess of scrawled, rejected, reworked, written and rewritten, arranged-just-so and finally accepted lines.

This is all I have of the earlier story – scraps, notes, and the resulting catechism, finished in neat and left for me. That was the last page written and the first any reader sees. It was brought forward: it's what opens the book.

I thought I understood it when I learned to read it: now, at last, perhaps I really do. If so, I have to decide what it's my job to do. I'll start with my own recitation, in answer at last, something important I've learned.

In

Keying, No Obstacle Withstands.

My second book comes fast, the noisiest of the three. I'm not writing it with a pen. My fingers quickstep on these keys and my second book rattles out.

When he met the man who became his line manager the boy was a child and naive but not quite ignorant, at least in letters, because of his mother's lessons.

Sometimes she would bring home from the town new things to read. Catalogues for grain and agricultural machines, and instructions for cleaning metals, and almanacs, or what was left of them when those pages making incorrect predictions and offering unhelpful advice had been torn out. All these in the formal voice of the language I grew up speaking, in which I don't write this. A few folded cuttings from foreign newspapers – which we occasionally found tucked between pages as bookmarks or secreted in stashes and which *were* in this language – we ignored.

My mother made slow poems of the words as she read them flatly to show the boy how the letters sounded. When later the man who would become his manager met the boy he improved him by giving him endless dull texts and having him sound them out, asking questions about their context.

His manager taught him that words change with time, by single letters or more, sometimes their whole roots switching – a 'y' to an 'e' in a name for power, 'sun-writing' becomes 'light-drawing'. The man eventually gave him this whole other tongue, and he revisited and at last learned from those cuttings about immense foreign wars.

The boy always suspected his father could read and write, at least some, and that suspicion was to grow. Back in the first days of his curiosity the boy found cards tucked between boards in the outhouse, little pornographic pictures with cramped handwriting on the back, but then he was too young to read them and he was never to know if his father wrote them or received them or simply found them and liked the images or if they were his father's at all. The old camera had demanded a long exposure, so the hand-tinted women and men crawled over each other in stilted and mannered lust. The boy put them back in their crevice and later they were gone.

He didn't know what if anything it was his mother got from his father's company. They lived together and passed each other every day and spoke a little to each other when they had to without viciousness or rancour but, so far as the boy saw and so far as he ever remembered, without pleasure or interest. From his father there was always a distant desperation.

His mother seemed always to know, and not to like it, when the boy's father killed things. It roused in her a cold and anxious distaste. That boy was afraid of her, but at those rare times of his father's blank-faced interventions he wanted the hurried and uncomfortable caretaking she offered.

After I saw him kill the dog I was more afraid of being alone with my father than I'd ever been of anything. But over the course of months every fear, however strong, ebbs or changes. My father treated me with the same flustered abstraction with which he always had.

Every day he was busy in his workroom. When he came up to the middle floor I would lie on the cold boards of the attic and listen to the murmurs of he and my mother talking. I couldn't discern their words but I could hear them speaking with a care that sometimes sounded a little like affection.

People might come to order keys. When my father went down to deliver them he always went alone.

When my mother descended, one time in three she might take me.

In the centre of the town was the bridge. Along its western edge ran black railings on which you could lean to overlook the foliage and rock and hills and the river. On the other side were stone buildings, shored up now with wood and concrete and iron girders. The bridge had been inhabited once but some ordinance had forbidden that practice, broken though it was by the parentless children who squatted collapsing derelicts between the shops.

Houses built on bridges are scandals. A bridge wants to not be. If it could choose its shape, a bridge would be no shape, an unspace to link One-place-town to Another-place-town over a river or a road or a tangle of railway tracks or a quarry, or to attach an island to another island or to the continent from which it strains. The dream of a bridge is of a woman standing at one side of a gorge and stepping out as if her job is to die, but when her foot falls it meets the ground right on the other side. A bridge is just better than no bridge but its horizon is gaplessness, and the fact of itself should still shame it. But someone had built on this bridge, drawn attention to its matter and failure. An arrogance that thrilled me. Where else could those children live?

They were a swaggering crew tolerated if their thieving wasn't too ostentatious, useful to the shopkeepers for the scut-work they'd sometimes perform.

Our town was a petty hub on the routes of mendicant salespeople, so sometimes you could buy unlikely commodities, vegetables other than the tough ones of the hillside, foreign bibelots, cloth in startling colours. The travelling merchants haggled and drank and showboated stories of what they sold from the backs of their wagons in front of the better houses. There were always small crowds at these performances, sometimes parents whose children looked at me during lulls in the patter. Even my mother would watch the traders' plays, or would let me: I was always utterly caught up by them, by *This Fine Borage* or *An Auger to Dig my Postholes*.

The sellers who knew her treated my mother with a cautious courtesy. When she approached, I silent in the wake of her skirt, they'd greet her carefully and might ask after my father, at which she'd blink and try out expressions and nod and wait. 'Tell him thank you for that key he did me,' they might continue.

A few turns east of the travellers' market, the butchers in the meat quarter sometimes stocked cuts from exotic animals and labelled them not with words but with photographs or hand-drawn pictures. That was how I learned that there were giraffes, from a sepia portrait on a pile of dried haunch meat. Once, one of our stops was at a large unlikely warehouse full of cabinets of salted fish come up from the nearest city, from the coast, wherever it was, and shuddering generators and the iceboxes they powered crammed with the grey corpses of big sea fish. There I, who'd known only the fierce spine-backed fish of the mountain streams and their animalcule prey, came to a sudden stop, slack with awe before a glass tank big enough to contain me, transported at some immense cost for I don't know what market, full not with me or with any person but of brine and clots of black weed and clenching polyps and huge starfish, sluggishly crawling, feeling their way over tank-bottom stones like mottled hands.

There were few trees in the meat quarter, as if the soil between its stones was too bloody for their prim taste, but elsewhere there were many, stunted to fit and strumming the bowing electric wires with their branches, always dirty from carts and the animals and engines which hauled them venting dung or smoke.

Southeast of where the butchers were, fronting a yard full of engine pieces and oily rags, was an iron fence past which I always hoped my mother would take us, because dangling from its railings was an angle of wood, a section of long-dead tree transfixed by the metal and jutting toward a stub in the flagstones, its own dead roots. There, a tree had once grown up and through the fence, sealing itself around the bars until it had provoked the unfriendliness of the owner and been cut down, leaving that part of itself that couldn't be extricated. That part I would finger at the join of bark and iron when I walked through where the tree had been.

The children from the bridge were often waiting there, eyeing me. They congregated by the stump and played a game involving motions as strange as those of worship. To me it looked as if they were feeling the missing bark for handholds, as if it were an expertise of town children that they could climb ghost trees.

My mother opened the gate one time and I watched in alarm as she bent to pick up a stained metal bolt. From there I followed her to where, in tangled alleys closer to the gulch, it was the architecture and not the plants that accommodated; buildings angled to allow for vegetation that had predated them, that then sometimes died to leave tree-shaped emptinesses in the town walls. I'd run into those nooks to stand cosseted by the bricks while my mother waited.

Little banyans lined one loud market street too steep for carts, smoky from workshops. The branches dropped shaggy creepers that, when they reached the earth, hardened into roots and pried apart paving. Locals would watch us uphillers from shacks tucked under the boughs, selling cigarettes and candies. Where they met the roofs, the dangling sinews hardened around their contours, so when those shops ultimately failed and rotted the trees themselves became open-fronted root boxes into which a boy could also step, to stand under ceilings of tangle, creeping down as if tentative and disbelieving that there was at last no metal to impede them. If you were slow enough, I thought, they'd turn to pillars and anchor you within.

Those bridge children would follow me.

I tried not to look too often but I could always see a girl and a boy at the front of the crew, roughhousing and raucous and seemingly fearless in their cutoff adults' clothes. I wasn't precisely afraid of them; I watched them with intense and guarded fascination, finding them inexplicable.

I had no money and my face was not winning enough that I was ever given anything free by candy-sellers. My mother stared as if overwhelmed at everything in the huts we passed, all the bright packets dangling within, with an expression that made me want desperately to be older for her.

A haggard man used one of the huts as a home. He lay on a sagging mattress, his head on his pack, surrounded by rubbish – paper, porcelain shards, food remains and unidentifiable debris. His hand was over his eyes. He looked like a failed soldier. Dirt seemed so worked into him that the lines of his face were like writing.

Beside him was a green gallon bottle, and something twitched within. I saw leaves in it, a moth's beating wings. A handwritten sign pleading for money was propped against the glass, a fee for looking. I lurched back as a saggy grey lizard bigger than my hand ran suddenly in crazed circles at the bottle's bottom.

Claws skittered against the glass like teeth lightly grinding. The bottle's neck was coin-sized: not even the reptile's head could have fitted through.

I ran to catch my mother. When I reached her I looked into her bag: she'd exchanged the food she'd brought down for other food, and rattling beneath those vegetables were more bits of trash like the one she'd taken from the metal yard.

There was a catcall. My mother and I looked up to where that leading boy from the bridge was in the scaffolding that held up a ruin. His companions waited under him. He let go of the girder he'd been holding, stayed balanced easily on another, shifted twitchily from foot to foot and watched me. He was short for what I think was his age, not much taller than me, but squat and strong and confident with his body. He called out again but my mother and I didn't know what to do, what response to give.

My mother looked at the children and back at me. 'Do you want to play?' she asked me.

I knew she wanted me to help her understand. Did I want to play?

She said, 'Play with them.'

She said she'd come to find me when the sun went low, and she walked away. Horrified, I cried out and tried to go with her, but she pushed me back toward the children and repeated her instruction.

I watched her go. The children approached: they'd seen her point at them.

That first time, what happened was that they continued their own games, always in shouting distance from me, a distance they made sure didn't grow too great. They performed their games for me. Once, when I grew distressed and made as if to go looking for my mother, the tall solid girl, the boy's co-leader, shouted at me directly, a warning sound that stopped me.

We were each other's spectators and performers. I got caught up in the gang's quick dramas, so thoroughly that when at last I saw my mother at the street's end below spitting streetlights, I realized she'd been waiting in the shadows for a while. She was standing with her eyes closed, listening to the bulbs' buzz, leaving it to me to see her.

I was crying at that moment, at some brutal turn of the children's game, and they were muttering to me with solicitous scorn.

When they shouted at me they called me uphiller. I didn't call them anything.

—

The girl was Samma, the boy Drobe. It was they who told all the adultless others what to do.

I learned their names quickly because during the gang's jaunts their companions would sometimes shout 'Samma!' or 'Drobe!' then cackle and hoot as if those names were curse words, as if they were bad and brave for yelling them.

My mother never spoke to the children. But by the cold kindness she could manage, when she left me for her business, she did so where I could see them and they me.

I'd rarely say more than a few whispered words to them while they bossed each other or wrestled or stole things. Even when they told me what to do directly, or when I obeyed.

'Chuck that bottle at that poster! Go on, uphiller! That was good! Right in the letter A!'

I adored them shyly.

Samma must have been fourteen or thereabouts, around twice my age, and Drobe only a little younger. They might have been friends or girlfriend and boyfriend, though I never saw them kissing, or sister and brother. She stood close to a head taller than Drobe, and she was fleshy and deliberate in her movements where he was nervy and quick, but their faces were similarly dark and angular and heavy-browed, as if they had been cut hurriedly from wood. They both kept their black hair shaved close.

I followed them on their runs and provocations – a little theft and the breaking of windows, was all. Locals would toss coins at them sometimes to have them do errands and they'd examine the money before picking it up, assessing the worth and debating whether to accept it for the haulage or cleaning demanded.

As the day closed they would take me back to where I'd

joined them. Samma would click her fingers for me to follow and walk me to where my mother stood looking at the men and women passing her by.

Once on our way we crossed the end of the banyan street, and Drobe saw me stare up it. However he knew my thoughts, he said to me, 'We ain't going that way.'

He was wearing a tall flat-topped hat that day, buckled from the trash where he must have found it. He often wore such a thing, or a bright bandana, or the remains of some studded belt, as if auditioning each item. I never saw any of them more than once.

'Drobe!' a boy hallooed behind us.

'How did he put the lizard in the bottle?' I whispered.

'That lizard?' Drobe sort of coughed a laugh and glanced away. 'Magic, mate. Come on, you don't want that shit,' he said, and he and Samma led me to a roofless storehouse where we could throw things around.

Sometimes her activities took my mother long enough that we were still in the bridgetown when the sun descended and all the nightlights came up.

If we were by the bridge at dusk, I liked to watch the children batting.

They'd sit up close to the railings with their legs pushed through, dangling them over the treetops of the gulley. A few brave ones would balance on top of the metal, right above the void. Though she looked too big to be safe, seemed almost too adult to risk herself in that manner, Samma always sat like that. My gut would swoop to see her. I could only glance, it made me so sick.

This is how you catch an under-bridge bat: take a pole of hollow plastic or bamboo, two or three metres long; wind old rope or leather around one end to make your handle; attach tough wire to it, or even to a winding spool if you have the skill, and thread it all the way down the tube; pull the length-of-the-rod's-worth of wire again from the other end, the end you won't hold, and tie it to a hook; then bait. The best bat-bait's a big flying insect like a beetle or a thumb-fat cricket.

The gang would lean out and dangle their batting rods and from their ends the cords would swing and circle. There's skill in attaching the insect so you don't kill it or harm its wings. And you mustn't use heavy wire. If you get everything right, your cicada, or whatever you have, will try to fly away and spiral madly in the air, lurching at the limits of its line.

At dusk, the town bridge wore a beard of poles and frenetic tethered insects. The light would end and the bats wake and set off for their night business in bursts from the arches beneath us, from the bridge's underside. They'd snap at the bugs as they passed. They'd fold their bodies around the bait to push it to their mouths – that's how they catch things – and the hooks might snare their skins. A hunter would bring each bat in while it jerked and struggled and hurt itself, and would wring its neck, then chitter in triumphant nonsense bat-talk herself, and maybe flap her kill's parchment wings and thrust its little body at her gangmates.

Sometimes a bat swallowed a hook. You'd haul it in on bloody wire emerging from its mouth as if it were pulled by its own elongated tongue.

The children ate the bats they caught and used their skins for many purposes. I didn't like the blood or the death but I loved the skill of their careful casts, the wrist-flicks they used to make the bait twitch, the quick smooth drawings-in of caught bats. I didn't like the blood or the death which sometimes put me in mind of other things, but I tried to dismiss those thoughts because the phenomena were so different, those children killing far more often and doing so with skill and to eat, or for a game or a dare.

It didn't frighten me to walk home in the dark, though I knew there were some nocturnal things on the hill of which we should be afraid. My mother always brought a flashlight to town and on those evenings she would crank it up and send its patch of glow a few metres ahead of us, climbing it across the stones and scuttling it over the path where it would frighten or entice little life. We'd pace toward it to the pattering of insects on its glass.

My mother was never so loquacious as when she climbed at night.

'I'm a southtowner,' she said, 'I grew up over there. On the other side, look at it.'

We rarely crossed the bridge. When we did we would go only a very short way into the streets on the other hill, where the shops and the people seemed different to me. That half of the town felt closer to a source of entropy.

I would risk questions. 'What's in the ravine?'

'Down there? Oh . . .' she said, seeming exhausted by my interruption. 'I don't know, I don't know. I can't tell you what's down there.

'I've been all the way to the sea,' she said. 'I was at the coast. There's a . . .' She sketched something with her hands: a tower. 'I was in an office. I don't know why they took me. They were training me: I was doing papers for them. I could still do it if you paid me.' She walked some more and said, 'I shared a house with a white hallway and glass over the door. There were seven of us lived there. It was close to the station. You've never seen a train.'

'In a picture,' I said. 'Which side of the bridge is my father from?'

She didn't look at me.

'There's trains there,' she said, 'where I was. I used to ride them.' She raised her hand. 'The centre was one thing, still carrying on, so you wouldn't know, but the city was mostly all broken down in a circle around it. Pretty much over. You know what the sea is? The trains go right by the sea there.'

'Which side is he from?'

She considered.

'Why do you want to talk about that?' she said. Her voice was flat and I moved away. 'He came from somewhere else,' she said.

'Is that why he talks different?'

'His accent. He used to think in a different language. He came to the port where I was working. He came by boat: he had to leave his own place, which is a bigger city a long way off, because of trouble there. He met me at my office. He told me he wanted to keep going, that he was only coming through. He needed to be somewhere smaller. Further away.' A tone in her voice gave me an instant's insight into what might have been their attachment. 'I took him here in the end.'

It was all the way dark now and looking back you could see how many fewer lights there were south of the divide than north. They were scattered. They sketched the streets in broken lines that curved across the slopes as if trying to encircle the bridge. They extended a kilometre up the other hill to the curious darkness of the generating station. I wondered if any of the lights shone on the house where my mother had been a child.

We heard the irate screaming of a town donkey, or a visitor's. I could see the guttering of fires and I imagined them in the shells of south-side houses, in the rubble, in the yards of the plant where the night shift was on.

'It should be all gone,' I said. I pointed toward the failing belt. 'Or all staying.'

My mother said nothing. Her flashlight lit me up.

'It should be gone or staying,' I said as I breathed out. My voice quavered a little and she looked at me. That wasn't unfair, I thought; she gave me such careful eyes only when she sensed this kind of particularity in me, as when a cloud of starlings had gone over our house with silent motions so violent that I'd run to her and tried to tell her urgently that the birds above us should have the heads of dogs.

'You take apart all the buildings,' I said. 'Take out all the bricks and push them down and set fire to them.'

'Bricks don't burn.'

'Hot enough like in the sun they do. Right in the sun. You make them ashes.' Bats, I saw bats again, but these ones I imagined in the bricks' ashes were as big as houses and not flying but walking in their horrid way on the tips of their wings and their claws, and the ash was baked solid so none of it gusted up at their touch. That was where they might live, the bats. Batland between the town and the hill, the country!

'Or . . . or pull all the *rest* down instead,' I said. 'The *middle* of the town.'

'Undome the domes?' she said.

There was only one dome in the bridgetown. Maybe there were more in the coastal city and that was what she spoke of.

Do it there too, then. Take the domes down and unwind the railways until the city was all gone. It wouldn't have to be a bad mess, you wouldn't have to explode the buildings in the centre; you could take away one brick, then the next, then the next. The grass would come back then. And the ring of ruin beyond would change again, change back, that very bit already gone into decay would unwind its decline. That's how we could help. In a few months *that* would be the city, a circle of revived towerblocks around a huge field of weeds.

'That's enough,' said my mother sharply.

I blinked and came back to myself on the dark slope, realized I'd been speaking, was quiet all the way home.

When Samma's group didn't come for me, I would accompany my mother through the town at no pace, hesitating under shops' sun-bleached awnings, acquiring pieces without any logic I could discern. Sometimes, to my anguish, she'd enter fenced-off middens, heaps of junk and rubbish at the corners of streets, and pick through them. She wasn't the only person to do so, but it wore on me as if she were.

There were higher and steeper roads where some houses were changed on the inside, rooms and floors removed, even, so the shell of what had been a cottage was now a church of some low faith, or a showcase for huge industrial goods. It was on the door of one such that my mother knocked one day, to be let in by a harried young woman in a filthy apron chewing flavoured bark. She let us into a dim acrid corridor raucous with throaty sounds. The windows were blackwashed and there was a low wire mesh in each doorway. Every room had been cleared of furniture and thronged with fowl, gathered by age and sex, tiny chicks chirruping pitifully in what had been a bedroom, larger birds jostling in the kitchen. I coughed in air dense with the dust of feathers. I heard the geese upstairs.

The woman spat toward an under-stairs cubby and two cockerels lurched over to investigate.

'Come on then,' she said. Then she said something in another language, but my mother immediately shook her head, and the woman went back to our own. 'What do you want?'

My mother bought eggs and a bird for eating. The young woman wrung its neck.

We went to a small stinking house on the rundown valley-side street. Its door was unlocked; my mother pointed for me to stay outside but when I heard her ascend the stairs I followed her inside, into a different reek from that of the chickens.

The house was a dump. People would enter to leave their trash and pick through that of others. Drifts of rubbish received me coldly, layers of mouldering remains, grudging hosts silent but for the tiny shifts of rot. I held my breath and picked through to the window, to join spectating flies and the drifts of their dead in staring out into the gap.

There were eyes on me too, from within a mound of refuse. The sight of them made me gulp a mouthful of that awful smell.

Glass circles in a hinge-jawed wooden head, nestled in the garbage. Years of decay had eroded its rudimentary features and drawn it an intricate and terrible new mildew face, from which I ran.

On a vivid day as summer hurried in I came down the path from the garbage hole and I saw my father walking up toward me.

I stopped. Sometimes if you stand very still and close your eyes you see rocks behind your eyelids. Or you realize aghast that the shapes of things are other than you'd understood.

'I didn't go in,' I said. 'You didn't say I couldn't go *to* the cave, just not *in*. I only went to the edge.'

I rarely disobeyed my parents. When either of them discovered me in any transgression I would shake, or I would freeze as still as a wax boy. If my father thought I'd been bad he might make me stand outside, was all, even in the rain. My mother might look at me and mutter with dislike and maybe knock with her knuckles across the back of my hand as if at a door: the painless sanction filled me with shame. Still, when it came time for punishment I'd always be paralysed as if they would kill me. I didn't move as my father approached, and I could hear only the wind around my face.

He didn't even furrow his brow. He didn't glance at me. I watched how he trudged, not tired. I looked at the hand in which he'd carried the broken dog that last time and I saw that what was in it now, what I'd thought a sack of trash, was a lolling mountain bird.

The hill was always busy with these flightless scavengers we called scunners. A scunnerbird is tough and stringy but there's much worse eating. Shoot one, you have two or three days of stew. My father had no gun. Scunners are skittish and fast despite their fatness and I couldn't think how my father had enticed this one to him. I knew that, by whatever means he'd killed it, it was not to eat. I wanted to cry; I stood still.

He had it by the neck. Its brown body was bigger than a baby's. Its shovel head lolled and its nasty hook beak twitched open and closed to snap faintly with each of my father's steps. The bird's broad feet dangled on the ground and bounced on stones as if it were trying to claw itself incompetently to a stop.

My father passed me. He looked briefly at me as you might at a stump or a broken machine or anything that's specific only in that it's in your way, to walk around it as my father did me.

I knew he was taking the dead bird to the rubbish hole, that he'd throw it up so it would curve as it had to and descend; I knew that day my father was feeding only the darkness.

The boy went to the low-down part of the attic where he drew, and drew a lizard in a bottle between the stems of the wallpaper's design. He came back the next day and, beside it, he drew a cat in another bottle and a fox in a third. He drew a fish in a bottle, a crow in a bottle, a mountain lion in a big bottle. He'd never seen a mountain lion but he heard them sometimes and knew he was to be afraid of them. He imagined that deep throaty growl contained by glass, and the thought fascinated him. He drew corks tight in the bottles' necks.

He cramped his drawings together to keep them a secret, and he saw that without intending it he'd drawn his bottles as if neatly lined up in some strange cupboard. So he drew a shelf beneath them, and while daylight reached them and cast across them the shadow of his own drawing hand, he put down the lines of a house around the bottles, to contain them, and he drew another house to either side. He could have filled the whole of the room, covered every wall of it in the smudged lines of rendered streets, that they could be filled in turn with women and men and children in the same lines as their city, some like small women wearing masks, some people squat as if they lived underwater. Someone there would be the keeper of those bottles.

He wanted his pictures to be secret so he kept that city and itemized all its citizens in his head.

I looked out. My mother was digging, and she came into view as she bent to extract unwanted roots. The wind pulled her clothes and tugged scraps of paper from her pocket. She balled something up in her fist and put it into the ground and covered it carefully and very gently with soil.

Soon I'd be too big to do as I liked to, to hunker and perch in the little window's alcove. I swung my knees up and braced them with my back curved and my head down, so I was bundled up on the sill as if the house itself held me like a baby. I sat like that on the ledge because I still could.

From there I'd look out and down across the edge of the garden and the incline of our hill, the rough up and down of the tree line, the sky. Sometimes people called it a hill, sometimes a mountain. It moved unceasingly. Branches spread, trees twisted behind trees in all the wind. Even the stone moved.

I sat up then because I thought I saw a new green, outlines of tough vegetation, neither needles nor fibrous leaves but spines on bunched and distinct knotty skin, misplaced amid the grey and those dusty greens I knew, swaying, pushing purposefully above the hillside growth at the edge of my sight as if deliberately positioned to be glimpsed against a sky the colour of the hill rocks. A quickly moving visitation.

What I saw was gone almost instantly into some dip in the uneven ground.

I came out of the window and ran down the attic stairs and out and up the footpath. I ran as fast as I could to the copse at which I'd been staring. I pushed straight into its empty centre to stand alone amid clustering midges. I listened for a long quiet moment, and wondered whether the gap I saw ahead of me was where the bushes and low trees had been pushed apart by someone big, or whether they were even still vibrating from that passage. The shale there didn't show marks well but there were scuffs between the roots, and I decided they were great footprints. And did the ground shake? As if someone had turned and was retracing their steps toward me?

Then the wind got up very suddenly and hard enough to make me gasp, so it was all I could hear, and all the undergrowth was moving. Nothing came back but those gusts. Turning, I saw two large unfamiliar flowers in the dust, bright petals right for a stronger sun, broken off in a clutch of spines.

I took them and returned. I re-entered the house. Hesitantly calling for my mother, I ascended the stairs, to stop, abruptly silent, by her empty room. I pushed the door, as I was not allowed to, opened it onto her things. Her bed was unmade. The few books with which she did not teach me to read were on her chair. Drawers and clothes and small pieces of trash were laid neatly on the shelf of a window that looked onto the hill from an angle that was new to me.

I could smell her. I wanted to stay and look at everything but I was afraid of her finding me there, and I wanted to know what it was that had passed.

My mother finished patting earth down as I approached her with my hands behind my back and she straightened and put something back in her pocket and waited.

'I saw something,' I said. 'A tree was walking.'

She didn't speak for a while. She stood as tall as she could and looked past me toward where I had been. Not knowing why, I kept the flowers I had picked up in my closed hand.

'Maybe you only thought you saw something,' she said, and paused. I was fascinated by her hesitation, the uncharacteristic way her mouth opened and closed more than once before she continued. 'Maybe,' she said, it sounded as if to herself as much as to me, 'it was someone from your father's city.'

She watched the horizon, her brows low.

'Come to see him?' I said.

She looked at me and though her attention brought with it an anxiety as it often did I could see she was not appraising me but a situation. She contemplated saying more, craned her neck again. At last she shook her head.

'You only thought you saw something,' she said. Her calm had relief in it and disappointment, so I too was both sorry and glad that no one was coming, to provoke her into finishing whatever she had started to tell. My mother bent again and returned to her task and I knew she wouldn't say anything more.

When she went in I planted the petals and their thorns where she'd been digging.

Two other times as I played in the dustblown slopes I saw my father heading to the dump-hole with the body of something he'd beaten to death. Both times I stayed very still to watch him. Sometimes in my mind when I think back to that he has my mother's face, or he wears a face that I can't bring clear, that goes between his and hers. But I'm sure it was my father. Once he had a small rockrabbit; once an animal so ruined I couldn't identify it.

Months passed between those times. If he did for other things, he did it when I didn't see him.

I had never seen my father kill a person, which I'm sure is what I saw, before the time I ran, but I think that was at least the third he had.

A young man came to our house. He was tall and fervent and young and well-dressed, one of the richer of the downhillers, I supposed. He was in a terrible temper when I opened the door.

'Where's the key-maker?' he said, jabbing his fingers at me. 'Come on, where's the fucking key-maker?'

My father came and banished me so I sat outside on the cold ground below his window and tried to listen to what passed between them. It was on its way to summer again and the earth around the house was garish with weeds, though the blooms I'd found and planted never grew.

I could hear the client telling my father his needs. He spoke in such a low quick voice I couldn't make much out. My father seemed to be trying to calm him. It didn't work and his own voice began to grow louder.

'Make the fucking key,' the young man said. That I heard.

My father made a brief response.

'You want a silver flower?' the young man said. 'Want me to give you a flower, councilman? Oh, I need it all! I need it all!'

There was nothing for some minutes then a grating sound and a regular methodical thudding began. I was still, hunched there, too afraid to rise, hearing the beat, feeling percussions through the house.

I don't know what name I'd give to the feeling I had – it was mostly fear, of course, but it had in it something of certainty too, the excitement of being not surprised, seeing myself there as if I was my own watcher, of discerning ineluctability.

The rhythm went on. I was blinking and quaking and I looked up into a sky now warm and heavy with clouds, and I saw my mother knelt with her skirt rucked to her knees, her feet parted in runnels of earth between growing marrows. Scabs of dirt dropped from her hands.

I looked at her and she up at me and we listened.

When my mother gave a sort of shudder and held out her hand I found out I was crying. She didn't sweep me up or whisper to me but she rose and stumbled urgently toward me through the ankle-traps of her vegetables and reached for me and I came to her with my own arms wide and she took both my hands in one of hers and walk-dragged me as fast as she could out of sight of the house, out of earshot of the impacts.

'Now,' she muttered. 'This way.' She kept making little noises. 'You, wait,' she said, seemingly to herself. 'Quickly now.'

She took me down the slope. We slid through the hill dust to a place only minutes away where I'd not been before, a fact that seemed impossible, but even quivering as I was I looked very carefully and really I don't think I'd ever seen that configuration of trunks and branches, that crack in the huge rock slab below us out of which burst an explosion of whiskered creepers.

A rock and forest animal, something quick and furred, bundled past close enough to show teeth. My mother leaned back on a tree. She still held my hands at the end of her stiff arm, so I could go no further from nor get any closer to her.

'It's like in the water,' I said finally. I pointed.

She looked along my finger and back at me.

'Like in the tank,' I said.

I was pointing at those reaching vines hooked and angled like insect legs or like the limbs of sea animals.

After a moment she said, 'Oh yes. The starfish. Yes, I suppose it is a bit.'

I shook my hands free. I climbed the ledges onto the rock to sit so my head was at the same level as hers.

'The water in that tank was salty,' she said. 'Like the sea is. You remember I told you what the sea is?'

She'd never told me. It had been in a book she'd shown me, though. I nodded. I was shy to look at her.

'There are fish under the sea bigger than our house,' she said. She narrowed her eyes into the wind. 'There might be starfish that big,' she said. 'I don't know.'

'Are there people?' I said.

'I can't say. There are people on the other side of the sea, so maybe there are under it too.' She rubbed her hands together and whispered into them, 'Imagine what they must be like. Imagine.'

'What's a silver flower?' I said. 'What's it for?'

'It isn't *for* anything,' she said. 'You want a silver flower, do you?' She said it nastily but saw me wrap my arms around myself and sighed and in a quieter voice said, 'It's something you give someone for running away.'

I climbed down and reached into the breach out of which those vines boiled and pulled out a tiny speckled egg. Within the crack a shadowed nest remained, and still within that were the remains of other shells, broken from within. The one I'd taken was dead and whole.

'When will we go back?' I said.

'In two hours,' my mother said.

I climbed down the steep side of the rock. It took me several attempts, but I held those rooted creepers and clambered down. I looked up at last from a shelf of moss and my mother was leaning over and watching me. She smiled at me and waved.

When the clouds got darker I put down the egg and came back up and we climbed the footpaths and returned to the house. As we approached I started to cry again and did so more when we saw the door was open, but my father stayed in his workroom, and he stayed quiet. My mother put me to bed and he didn't emerge.

—

Perhaps half a year after that, my mother came running up the stairs where I explored the great blank space of the upper floor. She half-led half-pushed me out of the house, took me on another of those quick purposeful walks in directions that I'd never before taken.

That time I didn't see my father. I didn't find him particularly subdued or melancholy when we returned. But I suspect from my mother's rush that this was another occasion when he killed a person.

The thought of my father in his calm-faced mood raised dread in me again but, again, not only dread: that time came something like a kind of muted happiness of which I'm not ashamed. In that moment, my mother took me.

I've said that the day I came running down the hill, trying to say how one of my parents had killed someone – the other perhaps – the children with their own parents were held by them to watch me. And that Samma was there too, and Drobe, and their friends, scattered throughout the crowd and watching from behind the metal guards around yards and like birds on ledges. One bridge boy hooted while I cried and tried to speak and Drobe threw a stone so hard that when it hit him on the side of his face it knocked him to the ground.

Drobe and Samma pushed through to reach me. They took hold of me and they clutched me as if I might get away.

There were no permanent police in the town. Every few weeks a uniformed delegation would arrive from the coastal city to deal with whatever disputes the hill people had stored up, to process what paperwork the occasionals, the volunteer officers, had incurred, the prisoners they'd incarcerated in our little jail. Until those agents arrived, the officers investigating my gasped allegation would be an anxious window-cleaner and a hunter wearing the temporary sashes that granted them authority. It would be a young schoolteacher with a faintly scarred face who would interpret the books of law.

The window-cleaner was a rangy bald man who gripped me hard and shook me. 'From the beginning,' he said, too loud, 'tell us what happened from the beginning,' and I didn't know what the beginning was. With which death should I start, which animal? Or with the look my father sometimes wore, as if he'd replaced his own eyes with clear or clouded glass ones?

The crowd listened as I corrected myself, wailed that no, it was someone else who was dead, my father who'd killed her, killed my mother in the attic.

The hunter came down to my level. 'The attic?' he said.

He was old and brown- and grey-bearded and very big. He put his hand on my shoulder and the weight of his arm was astonishing. His belt was a rattling bandolier. He wore a shotgun on his shoulder. He squinted up the path, his eyes bright between wrinkles.

'Wait,' said the window-cleaner.

'Fuck "wait",' the hunter said. 'Who's looking after you?' he asked me. I blinked and looked at Drobe and Samma and they looked at me. Samma extended her arm, not hugging me but encircling me without quite touching, and Drobe moved around her to stand on my other side. Thus they claimed me.

The schoolteacher and the cleaner weren't paying full attention but were remonstrating with the hunter as he walked away from them, his thumbs on that belt of cartridges.

'You don't know what happened,' the teacher said to him but he shook his head and raised his voice to say to her, 'Look at the boy!' He hesitated and took in Samma and the gang, who'd climbed down from their vantages and come quietly to join us, the gang that now included me. 'You be careful,' he said to us.

He whispered to Samma and put something in her hand, then started up the hill with the other sashed man and the schoolteacher running after him, he complaining, she lifting her heavy skirt to climb. After moments of hesitation a few others went to follow them, fetching metal bars and hefting garden tools, checking the firing bolts of old weapons, watching me where I waited in this new situation.

Everything, even the dirt, was poised.

Samma stared until, blinking, I met her eyes.

'Are you hungry?' Drobe said.

But I had no sense of that. Above us at the town's edge I could see the teacher with the hunter and his new posse, close to the outmost buildings, the teacher looking over her shoulder back at us. Samma shook me gently so I looked at her again.

'What did the man say to you?' I said.

'He told me not to steal your supper. He gave me money.'

She bought meat and grain and we stewed it on a fire in the last of those empty houses that the children claimed as their territory and we all ate there on the body of the bridge. In a big empty attic room with late sunlight coming in, that made me cry again, in a way that was new to me.

Take accounts, keep estimates, realize interests.

You can count a city in a room, in your head. You can be taught that, and if you are you might learn that you already knew how to do it, and if you do you'll have to learn to accommodate a new purpose, to encompass and itemize for a goal, to make it yours. With such intent, everything will be more concrete, the boundaries of the counted city circumscribed more precisely, and you may be more or less lost, or as lost as before. Were you lost? You don't have to know: you can go along with things.

I'm writing by hand now. The wasp is dead or sleeping. There's nothing for which my guards can listen.

Ultimately my manager would come to give me instructions, and I was glad to take them. And, unsanctioned, I was given advice, too, by his previous assistant, informed or warned by her of gossip among colleagues, a line, a letter at a time, demanding attention.

Something started in that new attic, as I spent my first night ever out of the uphill.

I watched the room with what light came in from the bridge. The house was full of the skeletons of furniture, around and through which the gang-members picked and played in complicated chases and which they gave new work to do. I was silent. They eyed me carefully and when they did I'd wait in alarm but none came to ask me questions about what I'd seen. Samma had told them not to.

At last a tiny crooked boy younger than most did approach me, so I grew tense again, but what he said, shyly, was 'Did you ever see that cockerel?'

Among themselves they said there was a cockerel made of smoke and embers that scorched its way up and down the slopes. They'd populated the uphill – where most of them had never been – with monsters. They asked me about them all – that bird, a scaly worm, a ranting spider – and all I could offer were the snarls of big cats. They listened as if they weren't disappointed with my gabbled stories, and the more I tried to say, to describe not only the animal sounds I'd heard on the hill but the beasts of which I was thinking, the more a guarded alarm showed on their faces with their tiredness, until every girl and boy gave up for the day and lay down on blankets or cardboard in cubbies throughout the building, window holes where windows had been bricked up, inset shelves that had held things.

I whimpered to think of the new stains on the old wall of my home, the glimpse of my father's closed eyes, or my mother's, their arms, those of the one stood over the other with something raised, some part of a body held. It wasn't my father who had died: he'd done the killing. It came back at me and I kept my new gangmates awake with screams.

No one punished me for the noise. At a certain point I stood up from the rag bundle where I'd been placed and recited one extended howl into the staring face of an imagined dead woman. Samma and Drobe rose and came to me and she picked me up and carried me outside. She was not so big but I recall no hesitation or effort on her part.

The air blew through me. I'd never before been in the town so late, though I'd looked down on it untold times. Previously I'd only ever seen streetlamps either unlit or in their initial fitful waking or lit from far enough away that they were glimmers like the arses of phosphorescent bugs. Now Samma set me on my feet and I ran to stand beneath the closest and gaped wet-eyed up at its filament like a visitor to a shrine.

In the generating zone on the other hill the unseen turbines spun fast to make this light that replaced the moon, against which the drop was so dark. The houses to one side of me and the railings by that obscured void to the other converged before me on the second hill, in the dimmer quarter that had once cradled my mother.

'Moth boy,' Samma said. She sounded fond. 'If you could fly you'd get right up there and touch the wire and die.'

'You know what happens when you die?' Drobe said. 'Do you know church?' he said.

I ran forward again, hearing nothing of my own steps. Samma grabbed me, held me as tight as a harness, but I still felt as if I was running for those southern parts, or then as if the night itself had stopped to pause my investigation.

Did my mother walk ahead of me? Even when she told stories of her earlier life she never seemed nostalgic, and I could think of no reason that death alone would change that. If she took that revenant route it might be she had no choice, that she *had* to pass through those familiar failing suburbs to scatter cats and go without a shadow past their hides in the roots of walls and carts sat so long wheel-less on their axles that they were less than landscape. To think of her made me afraid again, even in my abrupt nocturnal exultation, so the face I gave her was the sexless wooden one from the rubbish. With that she took the tight alleys in the shadow lee of geography.

It wasn't all collapse. Neither side of the town was ever only flyblown or air-bleached plastic or runoff and the slippage of industry but those were the castles she'd sought to live in, a cruder form, and it was by them that I considered her.

Someone would come to find strangers and those born of strangers, Drobe said, repeating things he'd heard. People had been sent out to perform such tasks, he said, to take number, and now someone was coming. I didn't understand him. It seemed I'd spoken of the trash head in my ruminations, and that mention had provoked him to interrupt me with his garbled information.

'From the same place is what I'm saying,' he said. 'I know that head. In the dump house? That's from when there was a time – where the counters come from – they were scared of all the engines and they smashed them all up. The ones that looked like that.'

Before we were born, rumours of distant insurrection had meant the ordering of destruction, the gleeless dismembering of all such geared constructed figures. One of a sequence of imbricated catastrophes our town had imported from the little coast city, which had itself succumbed to the anxiety, as we all did with so many, as a contagion from a vast other country.

Later I would come to understand that the doll's head I'd given my dead mother must have been left as a sole remnant of the moving statue bodies, a disavowable memorial to moulder on the tip while every other memento was broken and gone.

'First that,' Drobe said. He tried to make me look at him while he told me these stories. 'With the mechanicals. Then they had problems on the trains. And there was a war. Two wars! One inside, one out.' Samma looked at him, guarded. Who had been telling him this? 'Years ago. And it all ends up with people sent to take stock, to count foreigners. Like your father,' he said. 'Can you hear me?'

I only just listened. I'm surprised now by how much of what he said I remember. I wouldn't think of the murderer then; it was the murderee who had my attention. I was trying to hold her gone hand.

'Your mum's in heaven now,' Drobe said.

I looked down at the cobbles. He said it to be kind.

For breakfast we scooped clean our pot with tough folded leaves. While I was eating the last of our cold stew the officials found me.

The hunter came into the room. He walked slowly through the dust and the struts of light toward me in my corner. He picked a way heavily through upended furniture frames and children staring at him, mouths frozen open. The schoolteacher waited at the doorway, her face set.

'So,' the man said. He held up his empty hands as if to show me something, as I'd done when I ran down the hill. 'We went to your father.'

My blood went fast. The man knelt gently. 'Are you sure you saw what you saw?'

'Hey,' said Drobe.

He was in the rafters. Drobe would eat his breakfast half-standing in a high corner, hunched under the roof and looking down like a minor household god.

'You saying he's a liar?' Drobe said.

The hunter cocked his head and pursed his lips.

'Here's how it is,' he said carefully. Everyone listened. 'We went up to your father's house. Now, he told us that nothing you said happened happened. Hold on now, boy, hold on.' I hadn't said anything and I don't think my face had moved: Samma, though, was hissing.

'No one's angry with you,' the man said. 'What your father told us is you came when your mother and him were having an argument. He saw you but you'd already seen them going at it and then you ran away and so he went to try to find you in case you were scared. Anyway. What happened was your mother said she'd had enough of it all and when he came back from looking for you she'd gone. She went away, boy. Took a long way maybe so as not to come through the town.' That idea startled me. 'I don't know. That's the fact of it, is what he says.'

He watched me closely.

I said, 'He killed her in the top room.'

The teacher shook her head.

'We looked,' the hunter said. 'There's no blood there, boy. You know she went away before, your mother?'

'To that port,' I said, 'by the sea,' and in my head I saw the cracked and dirty window above a door and a glimpse of the white walls of a communal hall. 'That was before—'

'She wrote a letter,' the teacher interrupted. 'She said goodbye.'

I could only stare at her, her marked, expressionless face.

'How's your reading?' the hunter said. 'Your dad found a letter on the table, he says. We have it. It's not for him. It's for you.'

The letter said, *I will not stay here any more.*

They took me to the school to show me. I'd never been inside before: I was an uphiller with no money for lessons.

Drobe stood by the classroom door like my guard and Samma stood by me, watching my mouth move. The hunter sat me in a child's chair-desk, the furniture combined. He gave me the letter.

It said, *I must go away because I am not happy on this hill. I will go away. Perhaps you will be angry I hope you will not you might be sad also. I am sad. But I will not live here any more. You do not have to tend my garden but I give it to you if you want. You will be all right in this house your father will take care of you as I have I am sorry I must go but I must I cannot remain any more. Your loving mother.*

The teacher read the letter aloud. She saw my eyes going over the lines, she saw my panic and I think she didn't believe I could read. When she was finished the hunter said, 'So. Maybe what you saw was that. They were fighting. Then while your dad was looking for you, your mum got angry and she went away. Do you think maybe that's what you saw?'

'My father killed my mother.'

The man watched me. The schoolteacher shook the two big books she carried. 'He's allowed to confront an accuser,' she said, not to me. 'That's the law.'

'A little boy like that, though?' the hunter said. They frowned at me.

'This is your mother's writing,' the teacher said. 'Isn't it?'

It was a big hand of sweeps and curves. Some of the letters were nearly full circles. All of them staggered up and down and around the paper's lines.

When she taught me letters, my mother had done so with those pamphlet scraps, those cheaply printed books and stock inventories and instructions for machines. Occasionally she'd shown me ledgers and other handwritten papers from I don't know where, in various inks and in various hands, but it was only when the teacher asked me this question that I understood that every such piece had been written by a different person, or different people, in the cases where one piece of writing was corrected and overwritten with another, as I've done with a few pages of the second book that I continue.

I'd seen my mother writing many times but I'd never seen her handwriting.

The letter was on thick paper in a pale blue ink that I knew she'd used but that I'd seen my father use too, to render details on his drawings of keys.

'He killed her and he put her in the hole,' I whispered. 'He puts the things he kills in the hole. Sometimes he kills people and he puts them in there too.'

The officers looked at each other. 'Show us,' the man said. 'Show us the hole.'

They let Drobe come with me but they told Samma she couldn't. I think they were concerned she'd challenge them if she didn't like what transpired: she raged at them when they told her she had to stay, hard enough and with enough authority to surprise them, and that seemed to verify their intuition. They can't have known, as I didn't yet, that she wouldn't leave the town. As if to lose contact with its pavings would bleed her of something.

The three officers took Drobe and me on that long walk, the clough winding in and out of sight to one side, fronted here and there with wire, the tough slope of the hill curving away on the other. The hunter, then the schoolteacher, then Drobe and I, the window-cleaner behind us so we couldn't run away. As we entered the uplands I started to cry.

The woman turned and gave me a solicitous grimace. 'Yes,' she said. 'I know. It's not nice to see our parents fighting.'

The hunter called out, 'Show us the hole.'

I went trembling to him and pointed a way off the path to ensure we'd reach it without passing my house.

'Where's my father?' I said.

'You're all right,' the hunter said.

I stopped when we saw the cave mouth and turned to face the path below us.

'You're all right,' he said again. He conferred quietly with the other man and pointed him to the track. The window-cleaner nodded and went that way and the hunter came back to me. 'Don't you worry,' he said.

He went first into the cleft. He beckoned me after and the teacher nudged me forward. Drobe took my shaking hand and climbed with me over the rock at the entrance. Inside the cold shadows my legs were weak.

'Stay behind me now,' the hunter said.

The teacher and he went into the shadows to the edge of the rubbish hole. Daylight reached inside the fabric of the hill but that rip was perfectly dark. The woman shone down a light. I pressed my back against the rock wall.

I thought of my mother's hands hauling her up. Of her climbing all grave-mottled and with her face scabbed with old blood, her arms and legs moving like sticks or the legs of insects, or as stiff as toys, as if maybe when you die and come back you forget what your body is.

'You see anything?' the teacher said. She stepped back and shrugged.

'Look,' the man said. He took the flashlight and tilted it so the beam climbed from the hole as I imagined my mother doing with her face wrong and fungus in her hair. 'What's that?'

'No,' the woman said. 'That's moss or something.'

He squinted. 'Well,' he said. He turned to me. 'So.' He looked helpless. 'There's no way down.'

I made myself go forward till I could see white residue on the rocks.

'He's cleaned it,' I said. 'My mother must have banged it and got blood on it when she went.'

My father leaning carefully down with a sudsy mop. Soap-water wetting what was below. Down inside the hill, a second hill: a mound of trash and corpses decaying in layers and coated in hill dust in the dark. At its top, like a triumphant climber, my mother, looking sightlessly up at me with soap in her eyes.

'Why would he clean bare rocks?' The teacher wasn't being cruel. She didn't understand me and was trying to talk me out of terror.

She whispered to the hunter. He looked at me and sat cross-legged with the abyss at which I couldn't stop staring behind him. 'Now listen,' he said to me. 'So. My friend—'

She interrupted. '*Colleague*.'

'My colleague. She has the law in those books. You can't just punish people on say-so.' He didn't sound practised at this soft voice. 'You say your mother's down there. You see we can't go down there. So put a light on a chain and lower it to see? How deep does it go? How much does it twist on the way? We won't see anything.'

I imagined that glint descending like a star falling slowly toward my mother.

'It's what *you* say against what *he* says,' the man continued. 'And we do have the letter.'

'She ain't write that,' Drobe said. 'Come on.'

'His father says she did,' the teacher said.

'What if he said something about you?' the hunter asked me. 'What if he said you stole something or you *killed* a person, and we just said, "Oh, well then, if you say so, we'll do law on him, then"? You wouldn't like that, would you? That wouldn't be fair.' He looked over his shoulder into the black.

'She did write it.'

That was my father's voice.

He was stood at the cave mouth next to the window-cleaner in his sash. I saw my father and I couldn't breathe and I couldn't feel my hands. He looked straight at me and I made a noise in my throat.

Drobe stepped between us. Later I remembered that and I loved him for it.

'What did you bring him for?' the hunter shouted. 'I said we'd come when we were ready, didn't I?'

'He wanted to come see,' the window-cleaner said. 'What should I stop him for?'

'For fuck's sake.' The hunter shook his head.

'What?' said the other man. 'You got something to say to me? Say it to me.'

'I did, didn't I?' the hunter said. 'I said "*For fuck's sake*".'

'She wrote that letter,' my father said. He was speaking to me. 'We were fighting,' he said. He blinked repeatedly and I could feel his tremendous worry. He took a step toward me and I lurched back and Drobe moved to meet him.

'She was good for me,' my father said, 'and I was good for her too, but not in the end.' He looked beseeching. 'I'm sorry you saw it. You shouldn't have. I was asking her not to leave, is what you saw. For you and me. For you more than me even because you needed her. I know that, I know. I wanted to stop her, I'm sorry I couldn't. But you mustn't go. You *mustn't* go.'

He seemed to see Drobe at last, standing in his way. My father whispered to him, 'Move.'

His voice was sudden and different and cold and Drobe instantly obeyed.

'I'm sorry your mother went away,' my father said to me. 'I'll make sure we're all right, you and me.'

When he understood that they wouldn't take my father to jail and they wouldn't take me from him, Drobe screamed at the officers. Samma would probably just have got hold of me and walked away in any direction until they'd reached her, maybe hit her and taken me back. Drobe did shout at them that they were wrong, bastards, and so on.

I ran outside. The window-cleaner caught me easily. The hunter and the teacher with the law books huddled with my father in the tunnel and spoke to him too low for me to hear.

'We can't just take you,' the hunter came and said to me eventually. 'He didn't do what you said.' He said that quickly.

'Lock him up,' Drobe said. 'When the police next come they can go down there and look.'

'No one can go down there,' the teacher said.

"There's no one there,' my father said. He sounded almost too exhausted to speak.

I said something about the customer who'd come and argued.

'Smail?' my father said. 'Is that who you mean? Oh, son.

'I don't know his second name,' he said to the others. 'Smail. He came for keys. He was already on his way. He'd left, and he made sure he'd pass my house. He wanted one key to get money, one so he could travel quickly, and one for a disgusting thing, so I wouldn't make it for him and he shouted. But I did make him the travel key. Only that one. And he went on. Ask anyone. Ask his friends. They'll tell you he always wanted to get away, and he did. There's no one in the mountain.'

'You,' the hunter said slowly to him. He looked at me and said it loud, as I listened. 'We'll come back.'

'You should come back,' my father said.

'I fucking mean it. We'll send someone up and you'll show us the boy so we know you're treating him right.'

'Yes.' My father nodded with abrupt rage. 'You *should*. Look at me. You should come back.'

The window-cleaner was looking into the sky, at the waning light. Drobe ran to me.

'I'll come and get you,' he whispered. But the teacher was calling him and he had to turn.

The window-cleaner descended with the woman beside him. They still kept glancing up at the sun. Behind them went Drobe, watched by the hunter.

It was he, the last man, who looked back at me most, more often even than the boy.

There is a kind of thorned bush that thrives on the hill where I was born. I've never seen it anywhere else. It stands about a metre tall, with compact snarled branches that grow in dense near-cylinders so its copses are like low, snagging pillars. Its all-year berries are blue-grey but in the red light of sunset their lustre makes them shine like black pupils.

I stood among the columnar bushes watched by their nasty vegetable eyes.

My father didn't look at me. He dropped more stones upon a random-looking cairn. The townspeople were slow to get out of our sight. He waited and watched them and didn't look at me and kept adding to the substance of the hill with the substance of the hill.

When Drobe looked back a last time his eyes and mouth widened in horror at my expression. He would have taken a step back toward me but the hunter put his hand on him, not cruelly but removing hope of escape. The man whispered to Drobe and Drobe made some sign for me with his hands but I didn't know what he was saying.

When they were gone I stayed behind my perimeter of sentry bushes in the failing light.

'I'm not angry,' my father said.

I was full of the injustice of it; that that was how he tried to reassure me.

'It'll be all right,' he said gently. He stepped closer. 'I'm sorry about it all.'

I didn't move: I had no moving left in me. My father stood with only one line of thorns between him and me. He held out a hand.

And I was alone with him on the cold hill and I could do nothing. I stayed still as long as I could as if something might happen but it didn't, and when it didn't I shuffled as slowly as I could out from the vegetation, I dragged my toes against the ground but it was as if there was nowhere to go but to him.

He smiled as I came. He looked as if he might cry.

'Hello again,' my father whispered.

He kept his hand out until I took it.

His skin was tough and warm. I felt sick to touch it.

'Come on,' he said. 'I'll feed you. Come home.'

That first night alone with my father I sat in the kitchen without hope.

He cooked, glancing at me as I waited speechless and deflated like an empty bag. I almost felt too empty to be afraid until the night came all the way on and I lay in my cubby room listening for the sound of my father coming up the stairs, imagining him at my door, between his and my mother's empty room, looking at me as if I was something curious, looking at me and not at me at the same time. I stared at the ceiling that was the attic floor, growing dizzy. I imagined my father watching me as if I was something that he should make stop moving.

I don't remember sleeping. The next day I was slow and twitchy. I didn't know what to do or what was to happen.

My father would make keys. I?

'Are you going to play?' he said.

He fed me again. Put food in front of me as the grey light came up, that is, though I couldn't eat it. 'I'm working all day,' he said. 'This is for you for later. Don't go too far.'

While he cut metal I opened the door to my mother's room.

There were no covers on the bed frame, no books on the

shelves or surfaces, which had been swept, so there were no dust marks where any books had been.

I walked our home's perimeter of earth. What do you do on a day like that?

I wanted to see the letter again, as if staring at it might help me, but I didn't know where it was.

Several times that day my father shouted for me from the house's front step. He didn't do so angrily: just checking, making sure I was close. He would make me answer.

I drew marks on a rock with the end of a stick I burned for that purpose. At a certain point they became letters and then words. I can't remember what I wrote, which seems strange to me now. I wrote whatever I wrote, and stood back and threw pebbles at the words, looking for a particular parabola, an exact curve.

If they hit them, I thought, *it means I can go.*

The first throws went wide. I kept trying. When one of my stones arced up to land right exactly on what I'd written I felt squeezed inside, as if it were the writing that pulled the stones in.

He called me when the sun went down. One day had passed. I watched as the dark spread and I listened to him and I felt cold all over again. I smeared away everything I'd put down on the rock before I obeyed him. I left my slate, the stone page the hill put out for me, unreadable.

He brought me a drink of sweet herby milk while I lay in bed and he stared at me until I drank it. I hoped it wasn't poison. He watched me with desperate fondness.

—

I found the letter, folded behind a jar on a high shelf in the kitchen where it can't have been a surprise that, tiptoed on a chair, I'd find it. I read it several times and learned nothing and put it back. Sometimes when my father was not in the house, I would look at it again.

There came to be noises on the hill that were new to me. I thought birds of a kind I didn't know might have come to live there, birds that called with rapid percussive clicks or trod heavily and quickly over twigs or pecked them hard. I climbed higher than I'd ever gone to see if I could find them but the thin cold air and ugly trees and rock cuts diffused the snapping sound so I could never track it.

I ran and climbed as I wanted but every few hours my father would lean out and abruptly call my name until I responded, so I had to stay in earshot. On that hill, on the flint on which we lived, that was some distance.

Each time I entered it the room beside mine was less and less my mother's. I had a few of her books, but they'd been mine too, at least to use, in my care, by the time she gave me them outright by leaving, so I never felt I was connecting with her when I opened them.

The days changed and the view from what had been her window became mine. I climbed into its frame as I had once in the attic that I didn't want to enter again. When the wind made my house lean and creak at night, I'd look up and imagine that the sounds were made by my mother shaking the walls in the upper room, staring at where the blood had been, that my father had cleaned away. I still tried to keep her face from my mind, and sometimes I succeeded and she looked at me with my father's face or the rotting doll's.

Once as I sat at what had been her window in cold late light I heard two shots in fast succession. They came from somewhere on the stone slopes.

At the first I didn't even move; I was used to the sound of shotguns. What followed it, though, was a sharper ugly echoing crack like the amplified snap of dry wood. It made me start and look wildly through the glass at the flocks of birds as spooked as I.

I waited, but nothing more came.

When my father shouted for me from the front door I still hadn't left the house and I surprised him by descending from behind him, down the stairs. I was surprised in turn because two downhillers stood on our doorstep: a thin nervous man I didn't recognize with one of the ribbons of temporary office on his shoulder and a revolving pistol in his hand, and the sour-looking teacher.

My father looked at them, past them to the horizon for long seconds, then faced me. He was angry.

'How are you?' the woman shouted at me.

I backed away from the door and nodded without speaking.

She came in while her companion fidgeted with his weapon. She looked in my eyes and mouth and asked me whether I was all right, whether anything had happened, while my father watched and listened.

When they left she said to him, 'You be careful.'

He closed the door more slowly than usual, so as not to slam it.

When he ladled out supper my father said, 'Did you hear the gun today? That loud shot?' I nodded. 'Not heard that noise for a long time.' He frowned. 'Could be there's new hunting, maybe.' He opened the door and looked out while midges joined us. 'I used to hear that all the time,' he said. 'When I was in a war. In a city.' Not the nearest one, I knew.

The boy said, 'Who won?'

'High town against low?' the boy's father said at last. 'Street against street? Who won?' He looked at his son without expression. '*They* won. That shot? That's the kind of shot you use to kill a man.'

That night I ran away.

It was very cold and I put on my heaviest clothes to descend the stairs and step as silently as I could onto the flat rock around our house and onto the path, to come down that hill. I shook hard with every step, even with all those layers. I was dry and dusty. In the very far distance, in the steppes on which I'd never trodden and to which I rarely paid attention, lightning soundlessly connected sky and earth. My skin felt like old paper.

I didn't feel brave walking that path, though I had no flashlight and I strained to see by a slice of moon. If I'd stepped onto scree or braced against the wrong rock I might have started to slide and not been able to stop, and if there was no fence below me at that point I might have kept descending until I went over an overhang into a gulley, falling to my death.

By day there's rarely anything on the hill that would take you, but whether or not there are those things about which the bridge gang asked me, there are predators after dark, the nightcats and others. They might hunt a child. Coyotes and pumas wouldn't enter the streetlit town but they might have investigated me on my way to it. I don't remember feeling fear or determination or anything but as cold and as drab as the earth as I came down.

A clattering made me stop. No animal came, but standing in the dark where the path on my little mountain widened and grew shallower in the angle of its descent, I heard that percussive scratching. What I'd thought the sounds of new birds, closer now, as if something was bringing up gravel in short coughs. I didn't move.

On that hill, there were none of the true succulents of the desert, that I knew from pictures, that I'd once imagined walking. But there were spined trees, various clotted-looking things serrated as if with claws along the ridges of their bark. They surrounded the dark path and I peered between their spines.

Deep in a clag of them, I saw a human shape.

The figure seemed to approach me like someone rising out of water, a hulk of shadow with a box and a gun. It seemed to surveil me, and move without moving.

I hollered and I ran.

I didn't know if I'd seen anything real, because the hill will throw up its own nightmares, and I didn't care, just ran in great terror and didn't look behind me.

Nothing seemed to follow, but I didn't slow.

When at last I came slap-footed and quaking into the bridgetown it was still deep night. There were few people in the streets, dim but definite figures visible at junctions at work in their economies. They looked at me in curiosity. They couldn't have seen my face and it wasn't as if there were no ragged children in the town, nor as if none ever went walking in such forbidding hours. No one called to me.

I took a twisting route, striving for silence, returning to the bridge over the cut, to Samma and Drobe's favourite house.

My hope was met: the door opened. I stood in the threshold. My eyes were wide and I felt as if they might shoot out rays for me to see by. I stood half-in half-out, unsure how to proceed, and Samma opened her own eyes to look at me.

'Oh, you,' she said. 'It's you.'

She rose and came for me. She was sleepy and vague and she held out her hand and whispered to me with more tenderness than I'd heard from her or anyone, now it was only she and I awake and she was unheard by the tough brood she helped shepherd.

She whispered to you the story of when you came down, to calm you. You had a childish hope of sanctuary right there in that airy ruin but Samma knew better and pulled herself all the way awake and warned you, finger to her lips. She thought. She put her hand on Drobe's chest and brought him instantly out of sleep. They murmured.

She said to you, 'Is anyone coming?'

'I think someone was on the hill.'

Some other gang children looked up from where they lay at the quiet caucus. Drobe and Samma pointed them back to sleep and they pretended to obey.

Samma leaned out and scanned the bridge. A light rain now fell. 'Come on,' she whispered to you. 'Come on right now.'

Watched by those silent comrades, Samma and Drobe took you to your dismay back out into the night. You could see the lines of the country now, rising into quickly ebbing darkness, the hills' shoulders coming visible. Each streetlamp wore a corona.

Your guides surprised you. They took you left, above the bats' arches, to cross the bridge. Past that dark cart, as absolute in its aspect as any rock, into the southern half of the town. A street slanted up. They took you higher. Your skin was wet.

It was as if dawn had been told to come quicker on that side, as if the greater emptiness of the streets sucked the light in. What watchers you noticed may as well have been dispassionate observers from some austere alternative, so opaque were their regards. Destitutes lying but not asleep under leaves in a graveyard, marking you from their locations, cosied up to the railings as if to give the dead their room. In a chair by her open doorway a woman waited for the sun and nodded as your escorts took you past. You cried out because something terrible clawed from her mouth, a dark tangle, as if something hook-footed was emerging from her and she didn't care.

'Hush,' Drobe said. 'We have to be quick and quiet.'

To the east there are beetles the size of hands and their shells tell fortunes. If you boil them you can chew their dead legs, as did the woman, and suck out narcotic blood. But you didn't know that then.

'Ah now,' whispered Samma. She spoke in Drobe's ear and he thought a moment and whispered back and her eyes widened and she nodded.

Perhaps someone was behind you, glancingly visible as the town came into its grey self. You tried to keep watch of any watcher. Drobe yanked you so you lost your grip on Samma's hand and he pulled you into alleys, and you reached back but Drobe was too strong and fast, and Samma kept on in plain sight on the main way while you left her and headed into the snarls of the south side.

'She'll come for us, she'll come,' Drobe said, patting down the hands with which you reached back in her direction. 'She's getting things you'll need. Come with me.'

Need? It was light so quickly. Drobe rushed you in through the windows of a barely musty cellar. From there, when the rain slowed, through a fence of barrel hoops, by a junction past two big men in butcher's aprons who put down their tools at the sight of you and came after you yelling, chase instinct provoked by your speed.

In a foundation pit, the weeds were thick so you knew the building was stillborn. You hid while the men hunted. When they were gone, Drobe sniffed as if he could smell empty places. This early the sky looked like an ash version of itself. The air already smelt of diesel and there was smoke to run through.

'Samma'll bring what you need to go,' he said. Then in a rush he said, 'Hey, maybe I'll come too.'

I didn't want to go. 'And Samma?' I said.

'Well, she can't, can she?' he mumbled. 'She can't just walk out, can she?'

A big windowless brick hall rose on slanting foundations. Drobe pulled aside corrugated metal and led us into a dusty still room, where water and wan light angled through the ceiling holes. The floor was deep in birdshit and down. It sloped gently to a stage and a wall of ragged canvas. Things roosted.

'It used to be a picture-house,' Drobe said. I imagined what that might be. 'No one's here,' he said. 'Good,' he said.

He hallooed and got no answer.

'Whose house is this?' I said.

'No one's,' he said. He thought that over. 'Sort of.'

We steamed. He went to the stage and lifted a flap of canvas as gently as if it were ripped skin. Behind it was wadded-up cloth and a pile of other things.

On his knees, Drobe picked through someone's hide. He showed no surprise to find a box of papers covered with ink, some kept pristinely flat, some torn and crumpled, some printed, some handwritten. He touched them. Carefully he examined a stiff envelope banded with red, the remains of its seal visible. I went to pick something up too but he stopped me, made me lean over and look without touching. They weren't written in my language, and Drobe couldn't read.

'All right, let's wait,' he said at last. 'Until she comes.'

'Samma,' I said.

'Samma,' he said, 'or who these belong to.'

There were stairs to where bricks were missing, so you could lie on your tummy and look down at the street, to where a woman prodded a donkey past, dragging a big machine.

'You want to know who lives here for the moment?' Drobe said. 'A traveller. I met her.'

'Where?' I said.

'In the streets. She's a visitor. I ain't seen her here but she told me this is where she was and this stuff's hers.'

He pointed at the papers.

'She had a boss, but things went wrong. He thinks he's done for her but he don't know her. Don't know she's here, watching. She could get away and keep moving. She came here. He took her away from something bad, years gone, so it was like she owed him, she told me. It was all right for a long time, till it weren't, till she could read all the paperwork and realized things were off.'

I couldn't follow what he was telling me and I don't think he understood his own words at all fully; was, rather, trying to accurately repeat someone else's intrigue. Whoever slept here, he recited, was trying to find someone, not her boss, no, but someone who tracked *him*, in real authority. To present evidence of a crime. 'She could read instructions.' He shook the envelope he still held.

He pointed in the direction, he said, of the places about which he was trying to inform me. 'That way,' he said. 'They come from there to count.'

I had chalk in my pocket and I gave him a piece. He kept hold of the red-trimmed paper with his left hand to draw frogs in houses and people with wings with his right. I drew my father's keys and my house and me alone. The rain stopped.

'Samma'll have a plan,' he said. 'We have to get you away.' But I wanted to stay with her and Drobe in their bridge house.

I grew hungry. I sat and was quiet and watched the men and women on south-side errands swigging from flasks.

Drobe startled me by whispering.

'That lizard,' he said. 'They put them in the bottle when they're newborn or even eggs and they put food and water in for them, and they shake it out carefully to clean out their shit, and they grow in there till they get too big to leave.'

I stared at him but he was looking away from me.

'I seen them do it with fish too,' he said. 'Fill a bottle with water. Put it in there when it's fry. I heard they did it with a hare too but I never saw that. A hare in a bottle.'

He looked at me at last.

'Close your mouth,' he said. He was teasing: it wasn't harsh. I felt light in my head.

We froze then because we heard a rattle and the wrench of metal. We scuttled to a little balcony inside above the main room. Right at its centre, her back to us, watching the stage with bags in her hands, was Samma.

'Hey,' Drobe said. But before she turned to look at us someone shouted, 'Stop!' and a man walked out of the shadows.

The window-cleaner in his sash again. For one dreadful instant I thought Samma had brought him but I saw her face as she saw his and I knew that he'd followed her without her knowledge.

Two others emerged behind him: one of the butchers, his smock black with blood smears; and a policeman, a real policeman, from the coast.

I'd never seen one before. He was young and fat with long hair and glasses. His uniform was shabby but it was full: I could see the official sigil on his breast. On his right thigh he wore a pistol. His tour had brought him here. It was our town's turn.

'What, you got nothing better to do?' Samma managed to say as the men approached. She looked at me in anguish.

'I told you,' the butcher said to the window-cleaner. 'Didn't I say I saw him?'

'Boy,' the window-cleaner called up, 'what are you doing?'

'I said if you followed her you'd find him, didn't I?'

Drobe and Samma tried to insist that I was with them now, but the officer simply gestured impatiently for me to come. Then Drobe started on about my father, about how they couldn't leave me with him, and the window-cleaner grew angry and stamped up the stairs for me, and Drobe started screaming that he was done, that he was going to light out and leave and come by the key-maker's house for his mate, that he was done with this town, shouting so loud that Samma dropped whatever it was she'd brought to help me escape and ran to quiet him, and knowing how fast someone might withdraw the indulgence of allowing their presence in the houses of the bridge, Samma and Drobe, as he calmed, in agonies and protesting, let the men take me.

There were three other full-time and uniformed officers using the schoolroom as their temporary headquarters. They muttered to each other, they seemed edgy. They all but ignored me, except for the big policeman: he beat me. His attack was offhand and calm. He explained with passionless ill-temper that this was what I got for disobeying the law that made clear I was my father's.

This was the first time any adult had hit me.

The window-cleaner winced with every strike. I felt better and worse that even a man such as he counted this punishment unfair. He did not intervene.

When he was done, the policeman made me wait while he discussed paperwork and plans with his colleagues. I hoped the hunter would come. I imagined him pushing through the thickets in the foothills. I've thought of him like that often since, as if he's still out there, game in his sights, intending to check on me on his return.

It was early afternoon when they got word to my father and he came to fetch me.

I was sitting red-eyed and fearful when I heard a noise and looked up and he was standing in the schoolroom's doorway, flanked by part-timers in their sashes, a man and a woman I didn't recognize, and two of the visitors in full uniform. My father carried bread. His expression was solicitous.

He said, 'Boy.' He stepped forward and stopped when he saw my face.

My father turned and screamed at the officers, '*Which* of you *did* this?' in a voice much louder than any I'd heard him use before. He slung the bread away and it bounced into a corner where I eyed it. 'I'll kill you if you *touch* my boy ever again,' my father shouted. 'I will *kill* you.'

The officers blinked at each other in shock.

'It's those bridge rats he runs with,' the window-cleaner said. 'They been scrapping. We ain't touched him.'

'Calm down, mate,' said the officer who'd beaten me. 'Take your damn boy home.'

My father bared his teeth at them. I saw him compose his face and turn to me as calm as he could make it. 'They lost me your breakfast,' he said. He smiled at me. 'I'll get more.

'Come on,' he said. He held out his hand. 'Time to go.'

The shutters were up, the shops open, the roads full. Men and women swept away dust. My father pulled me out into the last few hours of that day – the square was crowded – and I saw Drobe and Samma and the others. They stood by a wall in my line of sight as if they might be there by chance. My father saw them too, and without expression gestured at them to keep away.

He held your hand tight while you stared at them. He rushed you across the square, disturbing greedy birds.

People watched him. He went to a bread-maker's and called for a loaf but the woman shook her head. 'No bread,' she said, and turned from him. There was plenty visible through the flecked window.

My father approached a man frying skewers on a big metal plate but he too shook his head at our approach and sort of reached his arm around his food as if it were a child that he was protecting.

Every vendor refused my father's custom. They gathered, they watched us with implacable faces, no warmer to me than to him. I don't know if he did, but even with my face still hurting from the policeman's blows I felt stung by the indignity of their shunning. I suppose it meant they believed me, but I felt shame.

Samma and her gangmates watched me and I them. They shadowed us as one at a time the shopkeepers refused my father, and all their customers folded their arms and went silent until he took me away.

What about me? I thought. *Can you take me? Please, let me stay.* But the law had said I was his and they had a lot of respect and fear for the law in that town.

My father didn't stare anyone down but nor did he wither under their disapproval.

He judged the sky. 'You'll have something at the house,' he said. 'We have food there. Good long walk and we'll build an appetite.'

As my father led me from the square toward the edge of town, Drobe motioned to me. He looked strained and he kept staring up and out beyond the town with an immense, furious eagerness, but he made sure to catch my eye, and indicated, as he had before, for me to wait. He looked hunted.

In the foothills, we rounded the last turn and passed out of sight of the main street. I kept turning to glance, to see a last glimmer of the bridge over the gulch with early anglers lined up on the railings ready for the first bats, washing flapping from high windows like flags. My father knelt before me.

'That's enough,' he said.

He shook my hand gently and made me look up at him while my feet picked over stones and the air went thin. 'That's enough. These've been bad days I know and I know you've been scared and you haven't known what's happened or what to do. I don't blame you. I understand. But this stops now. No more running away. No more hiding in the town. Or anywhere. No more. All right? You understand me?'

He shook my hand again until I answered yes.

'Good. There's just the two of us now, we need each other,' he said. 'We need to look out for each other, don't we? So. We'll learn. No more running away. Good. If you ran away again I'd have to come and find you and I'd be upset and angry.

'Now, you, come and eat. Those bastards in town . . .'

He checked himself. As if I hadn't learned from the gang any word he might use. As if I hadn't known them before that, from books my mother had me read.

And I did not run away again, though I thought of doing so many times, and made one more half-attempt.

Again I took to the topmost room.

As soon as my father left me alone, and too fast to reconsider, I took a candle and crept back up into that attic for the first time in months. And though I was quivering as I climbed, when I entered, even despite the dark, I felt no fear, no shock. Only a hollowness.

What the hunter had said was true: the blood was wiped away. So were my own drawings, which I'd thought secret.

The room would shake in the strongest winds, and I'd look many times across the night and the ruckusing air of the uplands and imagine being out in that, heading away from the hills, but I always stayed. I can't say I *chose* to stay as I felt quite without traction, without capacity to find myself or anything. A gusted thistle! That's what I thought I was like, for weeks. Thinking my own past self is mostly a mystery story.

My father continued to make his keys. For himself, I supposed.

During the daylight, I wandered. More than once, from far off, from somewhere in the steepening zone between the town and my part of the uphill, I heard that chattering call. I heard the complaints of animals carrying loads. Once more

I heard the *boom-snap* of those two distinct and distinctive shots.

I can't tell you what my father wanted from me; it may be that all he wanted was me. He loved me, but he had loved my mother too, and that love didn't preclude me watching him and waiting for any shift to come over his face. It didn't stop me wondering.

I can't tell you what he wanted from me because he asked so little. Now that I was back, my father was content for me to kick my stones through the fence and over the edge again. To explore up and down, to watch fighting chuckwings and rock rats hunting for worms.

I took a last few of my mother's papers up to the windy top room where I read them several times, or tried to – some were beyond me. Instructions for wall building; an allegory about selfishness set among animals; a description of a carved box that was supposed to contain a person's soul, kept in a museum, in a city of which I'd not heard.

Mostly my father cooked but sometimes he had me do it. He'd stand covered in key dust in the kitchen doorway, murmuring to himself. He would offer advice on what to put into the pot with what. I obeyed as if he was issuing orders. I'd always be quiet in his company. He never told me to take our garbage to the hole in the hill.

I didn't know how to tend the garden: I'd watched my mother do it but had asked no questions. All I could do now, with a growing sense of duty, was prod at the dry earth with her trowels, mimicking as closely as I could the motions I'd seen her make. I patted dying beans. Turning over the dirt, sometimes I would bring up trash.

Once I said to my father, 'Why do you want me?'

I still think that's the bravest thing I've ever done. I was outside and he was in his key room. I saw him as I dug and I stood before I could hesitate and I shouted it through the window. When he looked up, I thought for a moment it was with the open face, his blank face, but it wasn't.

'Don't say that,' he said. He whispered it to me through the window. He put his hands to his cheek and his trembling mouth. 'Don't. Don't.'

I wondered what would happen when we ran out of food. We had sacks of pulses and several loaves of the bitter bread of that town, which lasts for weeks and won't go bad. There were dry stores in the pantry, a tiny room in which I would sometimes stand and close the door to be surrounded on three sides by rising shelves of jars, of desiccated things, of salted bits, and, more every week, of cobwebs and the husks of spiders' meals and the bodies of the spiders themselves that my father would not sweep away except accidentally as he reached for food. So I would stand in that cupboard and see how the stores were decreasing. I knew we had weeks to go before all of it was gone but I knew also that it was depleting and that various staples would be finished soon, leaving us with those items of which we had a surplus, like dried mushrooms, which would far outlast anything else. I wondered if my father would simply refuse to address this. If he would make meals or have me make them with fewer and fewer ingredients so our diets would continue a while as they were but grow daily and weekly more thin, more flavourless, until for the months until the last jar ran completely out we would be dining on mushrooms, mushrooms for breakfast, soaked in water and salt, mushrooms crushed for lunch, fried in oil until the oil ran out and then simply seared and blackened in a pan over the fire for our suppers, or gnawed raw, until even they went and we would die, one after the other, the taste of mushrooms in our mouths. I couldn't decide whether I, being smaller and eating less, would die more quickly than he in this mushroomless state or more slowly. I couldn't decide which would be better or worse. If he went before me, of course, then I would be able at last – I can't parse or explain this logic – to descend to the town, and ask for food, not mushrooms, and to live. But then I decided that I would be so weak I'd be past moving and would die after all too, looking at dead him all the while, in that circumstance.

We did not die. One warm morning I entered the parlour and blinked to see that a large jar at my head-height had been cack-handedly refilled, leaving lentils spilled across the dusty shelves. That there were new pickles, and stacks of flatbread.

I don't know when or how my father was ordering food, which merchants were providing it or when they were delivering, but here in his hilltop house he was clearly not so shunned as he had been. Whatever money he had was good again.

Days after the appearance of the pulses, a young grocer walked into my view up the hill, in each hand a bag bearing the sign of her shop. She saw me in my spying place on a promontory. She hesitated, then sped up to make her sale.

Weeks after my return as I sat on the low branches of a tree watching my house, I heard stone knocking on the wood and I looked up to glimpse a boy wave at me from behind a rock. He let go of a handful of pebbles.

'Drobe,' I whispered with a great rush of hope, but immediately knew I was wrong.

I recognized him from the bridge house but I'd never known his name, and I didn't ask now. He was a slight boy between my age and Samma's, and he watched me with a sharp and agitated face, staying behind a rise, out of sight of the house in case my father was at his window. I climbed the stone behind which the boy sat and spoke without looking at him, for the same reason.

He looked around, unendingly astonished at the landscape. It was the first time he'd been out of the town.

'We've got plans,' he said. 'We're going to get you away. Samma said to tell you. We're working on plans.'

He gave me hard sweets they must have stolen.

'That's from Samma,' he said.

'Will she come?'

He blinked at me in guarded surprise.

'She won't come?' I said.

I had by then some sense of how we're all curbed by scends

directed at us and by our own compulsions, even something of Samma's own, but you must remember I was very young. Perhaps I thought my want would obviate them.

'She give me a message for you,' he said. 'Listen. "Some of them say they'll never take your dad's money."' He concentrated and repeated it singsong, as she must have drilled him. *Some* of them *say*, *they*'ll never *tay*, *kyore* dad's mon-*ay*.

'"That your ma's not forgot,"' he said. '"That they think of you."'

'What do they think of me?'

'Don't, I lost my place. Wait. "That your ma's not forgot. That they think of you. Help's on the way, we know what to do." We heard there's officers coming,' he said. I could hear when he went off-script.

'Officers have already come,' I said. 'They wouldn't help me.'

'Proper ones. Not the sash-danglers.'

'Don't you remember?' I said. 'They already came.'

He paused and looked worried at his memories. 'Wait,' he said. 'All right it ain't them then. Someone's coming, to help, I think. Samma knows. We can tell them about what your dad done and they can do something so you'll be able to come down to our house.' He brightened.

'*Who* is it coming?' I said. 'Do you mean . . . Drobe said someone was sent from way away, come to check on things—'

'Drobe . . .' The boy shook his head and looked away. 'I mean, maybe that's it. I don't know who it is he's talking about. The thing is with Drobe . . .' A moment passed and he shrugged.

'I just heard there's *officials* come to the town,' he said uncomprehendingly. 'And I'm telling you we've got plans for your dad. Samma said. We ain't going to let him keep you here. But Samma, she says we have to wait a bit, because if we just bring you back now they'll find you again like before. They'll be watching now, and then we'll be in bad trouble and then we can't help you, can we?'

He didn't look at me.

I wandered uphill. He followed me by hidden ways.

We threw stones at a stump. His aim was much better than mine. He broke off a twig with his first attempt and made himself laugh because now, he said, it looked like a fat and angry bird.

'Where is Drobe?' I said.

The boy wouldn't look at me.

'Where is he?' I said.

'Gone.'

'What?'

'He's gone. He left. He's gone.'

I stopped myself crying out. '*Where?*' I said. '*Where's* he gone?' I had to say it through my teeth. I wondered if my father had found him.

'I don't know. One day he just wasn't there. He'd been spending time with someone, then one day his friend was gone, and that was it.' I thought for a second he meant me but he didn't. I could hear suspicion when he said *friend*. 'He said there was nothing he wanted here any more. And one night he went. So now he's nowhere.'

'He's somewhere,' I said. I wanted to say more but neither of us knew what so we shared a sad silence.

When he looked into the sky at last and I could see him prepare to leave, the boy told me, 'Samma's been saying. You hear people talking about your dad.' I didn't move. 'They're all angry with what he done. What you said. Then after a bit you hear them talking about the keys he did for them. What they do. Like . . .' He cast about for an example. 'Like it changes the weather, one woman says.' He inclined his head eagerly. 'Samma said we might take it from her – the key, I mean – and see if it does.

'I mean, I wouldn't buy it,' he said quickly, 'I wouldn't give him any money for anything now, but if we could get a key like that . . . Well, I mean, changing the weather. Or anything.' He looked at me cautiously and shrugged as if surely I must see. 'I mean, that's something?'

I'd never used any of my father's keys.

The boy waited but I wouldn't speak. I didn't suggest he stay out of sight while I crept inside to see what I could find or that I'd leave the workroom window unlocked for him that night to climb in through. I wouldn't look at him. I said nothing about the keys at all. Eventually he went.

Sometimes when my father walked on the hills I'd stand in the entrance to his workroom and smell metal dust and oil and see some half-finished shape in his vice.

I don't know when his customers started to come back. At first I didn't see them, only heard voices in his room. First a man, then later a woman, explaining what they needed the metal to do. Then I'd hear the rasp of my father working.

We acquired two goats. One cold morning I woke to their urgent bleating. They were chained by the front door frantically eating gorse and butting each other. My father smiled at me and said, 'These are yours.'

They were young she-goats, frenetic and boisterous, and I loved them utterly and was terrified for them. I'd follow their famished, curious investigations of the slopes, the fervour with which they went for weeds, nosed aside a few fallen scarers my parents had made. I tried to keep them away from the dying garden with which I still struggled, a custodian of its decline. Whenever my father looked at them, I felt sick.

'What are they called?' he said to me.

I shrugged.

'Why won't you name them?' He was sad.

I did name them, but with fleeting, random syllables, which I changed every two or three days, and which I never told him, as if that might keep them safe.

They ate dead leaves; they ate gnarly barky bushes. They grazed on bedraggled refuse I pulled up from the vegetable patches, and on clots of moss in the corners of our walls.

—

On the hill we used a different, vaguer calendar than the one I've since learned. The seasons ours described – summer, dimming and winter – were suited to a different place: the mountain had two seasons at most. What we used was an inheritance, I think, a throwback from somewhere more changeable. It did grow colder in the top room. It was weeks after I'd run away, after the goats came, but I don't know exactly how long, before my father killed again, unless he hid other such killings from me.

I stood in the remnants of the garden on an evening full of sunlight lingering on the slopes, and below the raucous goat complaining I became aware of another growing beat. My insides clenched.

My father's window glowed against the creeping dark. He huddled within, bent by the sill. He was the colour of the dirt on the window. His hand was rising and falling in that deadening drumming, and I saw something limp and flailing snapping back and forth in his grip. There was no more killing purpose to his continued pounding.

I don't know what it was. He held the animal by the ears and punched it again and again into the ruined floor and made its body a sack of blood. I was sluiced through with a sort of bilious terror but I wasn't surprised.

Nor did I hide. I just stood by the glass and watched and whimpered.

When he was done breaking the animal (I don't know how he'd caught it, I don't know what it had done, I don't know why he took it back into the house to do it or if it was dead when he did) my father stood, holding the dripping skin. It was properly dark now and he stood in front of his window with the light behind him so he was a black form to me, a shadow man, and I couldn't see his expression, but I knew which one it was.

He certainly saw me but he looked at me no longer than he did at anything else before he left the room and I heard the front door open and I ran to keep the house between us and he went to fill the hole in the hill alone.

Once during the goats' vigorous evening meal my father leaned out and looked at me and said calmly, 'Quiet them, please. Will you take them somewhere else, please?'

Whenever he spoke directly to me I was pinned in place. I made myself stumble forward pulling at the goats' leads and they complained and went stiff-legged so I had to lean against them while my father watched. I strained. I saw past him to a man in his room.

Maybe I recognized him from the town, though it was weeks since I'd been there. I thought maybe he'd been at a pump, or hauling sacks of stone across the bridge, for workshops. For an instant, looking at the bulk of him, I thought he was the hunter, but he wasn't. He waited for my father to return to their conversation. On the table between them was a half-finished drawing of a key.

Are the keys waiting for you? I didn't want to ask my father but I wanted him to tell me. *Do you make them out of nothing or do you find their edges?*

He used scrap. He used beaten-flat metal panels, which he'd heat and into which he'd sometimes hammer fetish scobs. He used the blackened bottoms of saucepans: those he liked because they were flat and thin already.

So was there a key waiting for him to cut it out of un-key metal? I liked the thought of it but I never did trust my own hankerings.

When I saw them from that time on, some of his customers wore ugly expressions or put them on when they saw me, to illustrate how much they disapproved of my father, how much distaste they had for him.

One hazy cold morning he told me to play and to be safe and to wait. He put empty bags over his shoulders and I heard the coins in his hands and he set out to the town again, for the first time since he had come to fetch me from the police.

'If anyone comes while I'm gone,' he called back, 'tell them to wait outside. Or tell them to go away.'

If he girded himself to face the town that still despised him, though it would feed him again and used his cutting services again, he hid the fact as well as he hid many things.

I ran up the stairs to the top floor to watch him from its dirty windows. When he was gone there came a lonely calm and my chest loosened.

That was my first day alone uphill. I took the goats downslope a bit and they screamed at each other and I screamed too to see what it was like. They ravenously tore up what looked to me like nothing. I was close enough to our house to hear when, at noon, someone shouted at the door.

She was a thickset red-haired woman with a suspicious

stare who watched me with her arms folded. When I approached and told her the key-maker wasn't there she cursed filthily and threw something hard against the step, shouting, 'What am I supposed to do with this now?'

It bounced away. I waited while she stormed away and when she'd left I got onto all fours and found what she'd discarded. It was a bit of some engine. It looked like a heart, I remember that. I put it on the kitchen table. When, hours later, my father returned, he put down his heavy bags at the sight of it.

'A woman brought it,' I said. He picked it up and turned it over. 'She threw it away and went.'

'Whatever this came from,' he said, 'what she wants is a key to make it start again.'

'Can't she just put it back in?' I said.

Outside the goats howled. My father's eyes flicked momentarily in their direction.

'She might,' he said. 'She wants a key to help her. I could make her a key from this.'

I watched him sort his awls and files, his flat metal and vice.

He went down to town again, not many days later, taking the remains, and soon such a trip was nothing to remark on, and sometimes more people came up, as the woman had, while he was gone. And I'd tell them when to return. *I* couldn't leave, still, and I knew it, though not quite why. I could only go so far down.

One evening I found only one goat, though I'd tethered the two together, as was usual. I knew them apart: it was the more adventurous and argumentative which was gone. I could have told you what her name was at that time.

I picked up her chain. At its end was her leather collar. It had been cut through.

Her comrade seemed untroubled. She rushed up to me in case I'd brought anything new or unusual to eat from the cupboard, as I was not supposed to do but occasionally did. She eyed and shoved me.

I whispered, 'Where's your sister?'

Of course I thought my father had taken her but even then in the waning light, my throat stopped up with fear for the animal, it didn't feel as if he would have done this. I couldn't imagine him taking a knife to leather that way, not with his face as I'd seen it.

Still I could barely speak as I returned to the house. I told him. His reaction both reassured and terrified me. His fury made me certain he wasn't responsible; it made me even more afraid because he was furious, though not with me.

He slammed his hand repeatedly on the table and I made myself as still and small as possible while he raged at thieves. For the only time I remember he shifted briefly to his first language, in which I now write, which then I didn't know at all. He cursed and glared.

I saw him swallow and keep his voice quiet when he spoke to me directly.

With no gun he took some bladed tools from his workroom and went striding out into the twilight. A strong wind had come up and it shoved dust into the room before I got the door closed. I watched him through the window, flashlight in one hand, some nasty spike in the other, hauling over the rocks in the face of all the blown grit in the world, baying his ugly gibberish language into the hill.

I closed my eyes and imagined my house without him, without me, now that my mother was gone. Empty again, the house would grow more and more sensitive to weather, in the absence of noise, of human noise. My house had always known what the weather would do.

After I don't know how long, while I stood ready for something, I heard a single cracking shot, not far from the house.

Many possibilities occurred to me, with emotions for which I have no name. But my father returned shortly after that, still scowling, and the darkness became complete.

'It's gone,' he said. 'I didn't find it. You heard. Whoever took it is gone, and eating chevon tonight.'

He went to cut metal.

Long after midnight, with the grinding of his work still audible through his closed door, I came down and set out alone into the black toward the bridgetown for a third and last time.

I knew I wouldn't reach it. I didn't expect to be gone far or long. This time I didn't even put on extra clothes though I knew how cold it was. And though my face burned with it, and though my breath was fog, I felt almost too hot, or not too hot but too something, as if there was no boundary between the air and me. I was dissolving, both sweaty and shivering. I went without hesitation. I could see enough of the path to descend.

There'd been so many of these descents; there are so many ways to go down a hill. I remembered the last but one time, when I ran alone, a weeping mess with death behind me. That earlier me was a stranger child for whom I had care and with whom my patience was strained.

I froze. And after an instant a jackal yelled, as if it had been waiting for me to stand still. It was close. I tried to understand why I'd stopped.

A coil of mist moved in front of me. I tried to think about why I didn't continue down. I raised a foot experimentally and put it back again, slowly, just where it had been.

The mist beckoned me and pushed me back at the same time. It thickened and seemed to fill with watchers, or with a single fleeting man. I couldn't continue.

Is it his keys? I thought in the rising wind. My legs trembled.

It's his keys, I thought. Had my father cut a key to hold me?

I saw deeper shadow in that cloud and felt cold because there was certainly someone there, someone looming out of it, carrying a burden. I was sure it was whomever I'd seen, or thought I had, the night I'd last taken the path. I heard footsteps and quick animal breathing and the jackal howled again.

The mist seemed to move aside and be replaced and who came wasn't the dim watcher I remembered but someone smaller, a woman shape or a girl shape. She raised an arm.

Here was Samma.

I gasped and put up my hands and cried out a wordless greeting like an animal, and the animal watching us whimpered.

Samma carrying a bag on her shoulder come up so high, come out of the town I'd come to understand she would or could not leave, standing on the hill path ready for me, knowing I'd be there.

She looked taller and underfed and much older to me. She looked drawn so far from the bridge. But she smiled, and it was not too wary, and she waved me down to where she waited.

I thought of the jackal slinking away from our reunion. But I still couldn't move my feet further down the hill, so I raised my arms and, deciding she could overcome herself, beckoned her urgently in turn to come up a little more.

Another twenty steps for her and she struggled as if there wasn't enough air.

I whispered, 'See?'

When she reached me, first she shook my hand as if we

were adults, and I liked that. Then she hugged me in a rough way, hesitated and did it again, so hard I let out sounds.

'You're here!' I said into her clothes. 'How did you know to find me?'

'I heard something,' she said. Her voice was sluggish. 'There was a shot. Right near here. I thought that might mean something. I got thinking you might come down.'

She was lying. She must have been here when the shot came to know it had been close, which meant she'd been there a long time. I suspected then that she'd been up night after night, as far as, according to the constraints she'd laid, she was able, to wait and hope to find me. I'd come at last.

She shivered on the rocks and spread a blanket on the dirt for us and sat me down beside her. She had food for me. Sugary brittle. Vegetables you could eat raw. I gnawed them.

Eventually I said, 'That boy said Drobe was gone.'

We stopped eating. She didn't look stricken. She didn't look anything except calm and unhappy. 'People go,' she said.

'Why did he go?' I said. 'He'd never just go.'

'I don't *know*,' she said. 'He didn't come by you? I thought he'd come for you. What if he did, though? Maybe he tried.'

I heard sniffing: our hungry watcher had come back with a companion, it sounded like. We weren't frightened.

'You know,' Samma said. 'Maybe he did. Maybe he just went.'

Boys and girls might become more solitary thieves. They might find a way or a person with whom to become some sort of adult. They might antagonize the wrong someone and disappear.

'Maybe it was the police,' she said. 'He kept telling them to take your father. Maybe they took him instead.'

'What about his friend?' I said. 'He was waiting for someone in the picture-house. Not just you, I mean. Someone not from the town.'

She inclined her head.

'When we went back to that hall,' she said, 'when your father took you, someone had been there and took everything away except what Drobe had.' I remembered him holding that sealed packet we couldn't read.

'You know everyone in the bridgetown,' I said. 'Who did it?'

'I don't know. I never saw Drobe's friend, either, the girl he told you about.' She paused. 'Whoever it is has come to town now, they find you, you can't find them.' Her voice was low.

She looked away from me. 'I can't come back for a bit,' she said.

I didn't answer. Just watched her and tried not to let my lips quiver.

She told me she had the others to think of too, especially now. 'It ain't like I could keep coming back,' she said as if I was arguing with her. 'And it ain't like Drobe's coming back.'

She gave me a knife with a blade that folded into its handle. 'If he comes for you,' she said. She stabbed the air to show me.

She told me a few quick stories.

'I wanted to give you those papers,' she said at last. 'The ones Drobe found.'

'Why?'

'You can read, can't you? But if he still had them he must have took them with him.'

She hesitated. She eyed me and I persuaded her to say whatever it was that I could tell she wasn't sure whether to say.

'There *was* a woman,' she told me. 'Or a girl.'

Days after Drobe had gone, days since she'd seen him. Late in the evening, Samma standing looking out of the window of her second-favourite bridge-top house as if to discern where he'd gone. She'd fallen back in shock as a face swooped in to stare at her from the dark.

'She was like shadow herself,' Samma said. 'She whispered something. It was hard to understand her. She had a young voice. I think she wasn't older than me, or not by much.'

'Was it a ghost?' I said. Samma shrugged.

'What did she say?' I said.

'Like I say, it was hard to tell. I don't even think she was looking at me.' In turn Samma did not look at me; her eyes were fixed in recollection. 'Like she was looking behind me into the room for someone else. None of the others saw her. She sounded proper upset. I think she said, "Where is Drobe? Where's the *repeal*?" Then she was gone and I don't even know,' she said.

Samma took a big bottle from her bag. She gave it to me. I could barely lift its green glass.

'He left that,' she said. 'Drobe went to get it then left it. I think it's for you.'

In the bottom of the bottle was a scaly scrap and discoloured and broken animal bones.

Samma gave me a fast and surly hug without looking at me. I wanted to say anything to her, anything so she'd stay longer. I felt sorry for her as well as for me and, all over again, I didn't want to be alone on the hill with my father. But I couldn't stop her.

'I'll come when I can,' she said and went quickly back to the path. She tried not to let me see her relief as she descended.

You wanted to put your foot down after her, but you didn't, maybe couldn't. You watched her go.

That was the last time you saw her. The cold return, the lights of your father's room, the dark formlessness of the house waited.

A man came.

My father had gone downhill. I was upstairs, drawing on the walls, to repopulate them at last. The animals I drew looked different now. I added faces and stood them upright. The new arrivals eyed the streets where their predecessors had been and I whispered to them all. I could feel the house buck in the gusts, and through the windows I saw trees hurled around.

Someone knocked and I started so violently I hurt my neck. But I knew it wasn't my father so I ran down the stairs and opened the door.

Strips of leaf and twigs rushed into the kitchen. I braced. The sky was all flat cloud but bright. I was looking into a silhouette. I blinked to clear the wind from my eyes.

'The key-maker's not here,' I said. 'You can wait outside. I don't know how long he'll be. Or you can go back to the town and he'll be here again tomorrow.'

'I'm not here for the key-maker,' the visitor said.

I could see his outlines now. A man who held something in his hands.

His skin was deeply lined, but I don't think he was much older than my father. He was bald but for an island of short grey hair at the front of his forehead and a rim of it at the back of his head. He was tall, not as rangy as my father but thin and tough looking. He wore glasses. The reflections on their lenses hid his eyes. He had on a dark grey suit with a white shirt. All his clothes were dusty. The bridgetown people didn't wear ties and I was bewildered by the stripe of black-blue cloth criss-crossed with a simple design.

He carried a big rifle over his shoulder, a box in his left hand, a clipboard in his right.

The man reared back his head and I saw that his spectacles were made of shifting planes. I'd never seen such machines as bifocals. He looked at me through the magnifying facets.

'He isn't here,' I repeated.

'I'm not here to speak to him,' the man said. He spoke with a kind of singsong enthusiasm. He used my language well but I could tell it wasn't his own. 'That is, I am, eventually,' he said. 'I will. He'll be back. It's very much my job to speak to him. But I came here now because he isn't here.'

His accent was familiar to me.

He said, 'I came to speak to you.'

I didn't let him into the house and he didn't ask to enter. He put down the leather box-suitcase. He held his papers flat against his body. Below us on the slope I could see a swirl of dark frozen air, a hillside squall throwing one of the brief year-round bursts of snow that characterizes that region. It sounded like voices.

'So, I *am* here to speak to your father,' the visitor said. 'But not yet. I have to do a job. I will be asking him questions. I've been working in the town, and I've kept hearing about things that I need to follow up. That I need to know more about.' He looked at me carefully until I lowered my eyes.

A guffaw shocked me.

'My mule,' the man said. He pointed down the hill to where my own unseen goat was answering his animal.

'I have to make a record,' he said. 'I'm here because I need information from certain people in town. Your father's one of them, because of where he was born. So I need to know things. Like what he does.'

'We're not in town,' I mumbled.

'This counts as town.'

'I can tell you what he does,' I said.

'What money he makes,' he continued. 'How long he's been here. Where he was born I *know*. Which is the point.'

I shifted.

'What he did back there. At different times, good, and not good. People in town have told me a lot about this and that's all very well but I do need to know from him. He's the last subject here, but one. This is the last household. I need to know about his family.' He tilted his head. 'Which means I have to know about his children, and I'm going to ask him about them. Which means you. Yes.

'And,' he said, 'I have to ask him about his wife.'

'You know,' I said instantly.

'What's that?'

'You *know*.' I dredged it out. 'They said. Down there. They *told* you. About my mother.'

'Below?' He didn't look away from me. 'They did.' I strained to hear. 'They did tell me things but I do need to know for certain. I need to hear from the key-maker himself. And his family.'

'You know she's gone.'

I stretched up on tiptoe and looked past him down the

rocks. The tiny storm was done. They last only seconds, and if you're caught in them their snowflakes are so minuscule and dry they feel like cold dust.

The man's weapon had two barrels and they were not the same. One was thick enough that I could have put two of my fingers into it, the other perhaps half that bore.

'This?' he said. He took it from his shoulder and held it for me to see. 'It's a combination gun. Look, two triggers. This' – he tapped the broad-gauge tube – 'is a shotgun. It spreads possibilities.' He made an extending cone with his hands. 'And this?' The other. 'This rifle's a long-range single shot.'

He showed me how he'd aim with it.

'You can shoot one, the other, or both. The rifle shoots right down the very centre of the spread. Like an average. A range and its mean. This is an averaging gun.'

He shouldered it carefully again.

'They said your father's wife is gone, yes, that's what they said to me,' the man said. He held his pen above his clipboard. 'We can get started,' he said. 'We can save time. You tell me about it.'

And I who months before had run into town screaming my accusation was shy to say it now that I was asked to put it in clear words. I'd grown used to this world in which everyone knew what had happened or what I said had, in which it had gone from being spoken to being unspoken again, a secret everybody knew. Here I was, hesitating to speak it. I took persuading. The foreign man would have to work on me.

He waited with his pen ready. He said to me, 'What I do is I count people. I count people and things.

'Not everyone. If you counted everyone you'd never stop, would you? I'm putting things in sets. My job's to count just the people who were born where I was, or whose parents or grandparents were. Then I write down what I've counted. That's my job. I started years ago, when we decided we had to take stock of things. After troubles. We needed to know where we were. Where we all were. So I go all over counting people from my home. I'll show you where I put it all. There are books.

'Your father came here a long time ago and he's my responsibility. I have to mark his details, you see. I *know* you were born here. If I'm marking down about him that means I have to mark down something about you. And something about your mother. I have to get the details right. There aren't many in this town who come from where I do, but there are a few. One's a poultry farmer. She told me there was one more person of my polity up here. On this job, yours is the last family I have to account for.'

I told him what my father had done.

I told him what he'd done not only to my mother but to the others, to the people and the animals. I told the man as he stood on my front step in the leaf-dust, disallowed from the house because my father had forbidden me to let anyone in.

The visitor listened. I couldn't see what he wrote down.

I don't know if my voice shifted up and down with hope and desperation. I didn't know when my father would come home. I wouldn't look in the direction he'd taken, nor would I step forward to see the path, with him perhaps rising on it now. I told it all again.

It must have been confused and it must have taken a while. I sat cross-legged in the threshold and kept talking. The man stood and wrote. Twice his mule called for him and he ignored it.

I didn't tell the story to ask for help because I knew there was no help. I told the man because he asked me to, because that was what he said he wanted. For his notes.

'Where was she from?' he said.

I shook my head. I was crying a bit by then, without noise.

'From here,' I said. 'But she went to live by the sea. That's where they met. I have something she wrote. But I don't think she wrote it. D'you want to see?'

'I do.'

'I'll get it for you.'

'You told all this to the people in the town,' he said.

'They said they can't do anything because of no proof.'

He looked up and said, 'Do you know why your father ran here in the first place? I know. Where do *you* think your mother is?' He said that quietly and didn't lower his clipboard.

My voice caught and it took several attempts to answer.

'In the hole,' I said.

'In the hole. Maybe you can show me the hole.'

I did nothing and he regarded me.

'You remember the job I have to do?' he said. 'You remember I need to write down everything I can about your mother? So I should see what there is to see so I can get all my details right.

'Show me.'

—

I took him to the rubbish hole.

We went around the house and up onto the rough ground between thorns and dock bushes and a few metres beyond the closest trees I passed by where I'd buried the bottle with the skeleton still inside.

Looking back I saw the roan mule on the path. A big animal laden under packs. It looked up as we came into its sightline and put back its ears and huffed at us as we ascended.

I stood at the cave mouth's rocky stockade and gestured within.

The man entered. He walked in and stopped where the crack split the darkness of the cave with a darker cut. He leaned carefully over as the hunter and the schoolteacher and my mother and father had done.

He got onto his hands and knees and gripped the edge and lowered his head into the rift. I watched him with my hands held tightly to my chest.

I said, 'It goes on down.'

'It does,' he said. He didn't turn to me and his voice was faint. He was speaking into the dark.

'No one can see inside,' I said. 'No one can see down there.'

'Well,' he said. He rose. He turned and came back into the day brushing dirt off his knees and the palms of his hands. 'I have to be sure, that's part of my job. So let me see.'

When he left me there I was too surprised to be afraid as he walked briskly back the way we had come. I didn't know if I was wanted so I waited and he quickly returned carrying a satchel.

'One thing I do have to count,' he said, 'is spouses.'

He took out a tube of glass or clear plastic the size of a hammer handle and pressed something, shook it, and the cylinder glowed. It went quickly, coldly bright.

I climbed over the entrance rocks and came into the cave toward him.

The man held out the stick of light and dropped it into the hole.

I gasped to see it plummet, fleetingly illuminating the jagged rock sides, dwindling, knocking loudly end to end on the stone until it was invisible.

We watched. The man exhaled.

He took out a flashlight, thick rope, hooks and spikes and buckled leather for his chest, into which he shrugged. I watched with some growing emotion.

'No one can go down,' I said.

'Yes, well, I have a job,' he said. He hammered clasps into the rock. 'I have to count. I have to track everything.'

He attached hooks and the cord to these anchors. He spooled it around his harness.

'You can't,' I said desperately. 'You can't.'

'Do you know how you could help me?' he said. 'You know what I need? You should listen. Can you do that? Listen as hard as you can. And if anyone's coming you should shout down and tell me.'

He gave me another of the tubes. It was pleasing and heavy in my hand. I could see two just-distinct clear liquids inside. 'If you hear anyone, you press this.' A plunger to crack the wall between the chambers. 'Can you do that? Then you shake it and drop it right in.'

'What if I hit you?'

'Then I'll have a bump on my head.' He made a silly face.

'What if it breaks on the rocks?' He shook his head and tapped it on the rock to show me it was tough.

'But you won't turn it on unless you hear someone?' he said.

I promised.

He took his glasses off and cleaned them and put them on again. He wound the strap of his flashlight around his wrist.

'Let's see,' he said. 'Well, now.'

Spooling out the line, the man stepped over the lip into the hole.

He moved fast, keeping the line taut with one arm while he braced himself expertly against outcroppings and in nooks with the other and with his legs, and scuttled down the stone.

The dark took him. I watched the line tremble and stretch.

I watched his glow go down.

I couldn't hear him any more but for a minute his light switched back and forth in the pit, once shining right up out of it and into my eyes. Then he turned it off or passed below an overhang.

The cord thrummed.

In my mind I saw him, a tiny figure suspended and sinking in a great chamber toward the pile. I imagined him shining his light down at it.

I thought there might be sounds from the hill path outside. I was afraid. That my father was returning.

And I imagined the man touching down on the dreadful hill inside the hill and I thought of what I would do if my father came and found me now, waiting there, and of what he might do. I started to shake as if I was frozen cold. I didn't know whether because of the thought of what the man would find or of the thought of my father finding me.

If my father said something, what would I say back?

I'd try hard not to look at the line stretching down. I'd keep my eyes from the hole. But that wouldn't distract him. He would see the line. He'd look straight at it and a terrible expression would come over him, not the calm he wore when killing but anger that there was an intruder and a great determination not to let the man have the knowledge for which he was searching, and my father would pull a knife from his pocket and go toward the cord to cut it.

So would I struggle with him? He would throw me down into the gap if I did, killing me in a new rageful way. I resolved that I *would* struggle with him, that I'd try to stop his knife and give the man time to come up again. I was afraid that I wouldn't be brave enough.

I stood alone and held the tube, ready to make it glow, ready to drop it.

There were animals close by and I could hear the sounds of the hillside but, though I thought I did, many times, I didn't hear my father returning. I stood in the cave for minutes, for an hour, for more than an hour. I watched the daylight change outside.

Down in the ground, perhaps the man climbed. Or did he dig?

I stared at nothing in the shadow in the hill. I was racked by scenes, moments that I didn't want to imagine, the man's story now, his under-hill investigations. I wanted not to imagine anything like the whispering and snarling dead who filled my head, dead people clotting in a great pile, sliding over the house trash like a band of murdered animals gone blind and stupid with rage in the darkness, furious with anyone still alive, a familiar figure at their head.

The stretched cord's noises, its creaks and snaps, changed. It vibrated more quickly. The man was ascending.

I pictured him bracing. Climbing.

'Quick,' I struggled to whisper, into the hole. I spoke in a tiny voice. 'I think my father's coming. I keep hearing noises. You have to hurry.'

No light came up. The man had been in darkness down there, and he was ascending in the darkness.

The man was ascending, I thought, and then I thought, *What if the man isn't ascending?*

What if it isn't him rising?

How long might they have been waiting down there? Waiting to overpower whoever brought a way out, ingrate escapees. Little sounds welled out of my throat and the black welled up out of the gap. The light-tube shook in my grip.

I knew who would climb first, who would be at the front of the mass, whose ruined fingers and nails it would be slapping onto the sharp flint at the edges of the crack, who would rise out of the under-hill to meet my eye, whose cold grave-stained face full of disappointment.

But it was the foreign man who came into my view like a fish below a boat. I saw him when he was already close to me. He turned his face up and I saw it paler than the shadow.

He gathered the cord and gripped the rock and found handholds. I couldn't believe that he was returning.

The man hauled himself at last out of the ground, lying at the cut's edge, panting and staring around him and blinking quickly. I could smell no miasma on him.

After a while he pulled a cloth from his pocket and wiped his hands very carefully, then his face. He took off his glasses and cleaned them again and wouldn't look at me. His clothes were coated in dust from under the world.

He gathered himself and shrugged out of his harness. I couldn't speak and he said nothing. His face was set. He worked his jaw.

'I heard what you said to me,' he said at last. 'When I was on my way up. Your father *will* come home soon, I think.'

He put everything back in his sack.

'I think you shouldn't go back to the house,' he said. He still didn't look at me. 'You know I have to do this job. I want to speak to your father now. I think it would be better if we could speak alone.'

—

'You can't go in,' I whispered. 'It's not allowed.'

'I know,' he said. 'I'll wait for him outside. I promise I'll stay on the step.' He kept looking at the cave mouth. 'I'll wait for him and ask him if *he'll* let me come inside. And if he won't I'll talk to him right there. But I want you to stay here, now. All right?'

He looked across the hole at the dark of the hollow beyond, and back at me at last, at my little limbs.

'Well,' he said. 'Is there somewhere you can go? Quiet? Out of sight? Just to make sure your father doesn't . . .' He put his finger to his lips. 'I want you to stay quiet. Keep your ears open, I can call you after I've asked your father those questions.'

'I'll find somewhere.' I was wondering about the crook of a tree, some bough.

'Where you can't be seen?' he said. 'Make sure it's not too close.'

His insistence frightened me. I couldn't sit anywhere in the dusk for my father to see me watching. 'I don't know,' I said. But he was distracted, so I said, 'I'll find a place.'

'Good.' He nodded. He picked up his pack and walked into the last of the afternoon. I followed, screwing up my eyes. But as I watched him stride out of sight down the hill I stopped, still within the cave mouth.

These felt very much like last moments. And I was very tired and I didn't want the light on me.

Had I been in the house I would have gone into the parlour and closed the door. Or I would have wrapped old sheets around me in the base of a wardrobe. I couldn't go back to the house.

The hole watched me, above its discards and the insides

of the hill. Despite what it contained, I took a step back toward it.

It wasn't my friend or my enemy. It was only a rip full of stone and old things. Even with a particular thing. I didn't want it but I didn't need to run from it, not then, and I was afraid of it but no more than I was afraid of everything. Just then, before the conversation between the stranger and my father, I was less afraid of it than of stepping out into the light.

I walked back toward the blackness. I whispered into it, in case my mother was listening.

If he came in here my father would see me and reach for me. I threw a stone across the wide split to the ridge beyond.

With as long a run-up as I could take I might be able to jump all the way across, but the floor was uneven and I might trip on my way and pitch forward, or reach the other side but tip back, and go down, into the dark to the other peak.

The cave wall had its handholds. Outside the sun was firing up the flanks of the hill and somewhere on them my father was coming back to the house, where by the front door the man in his dusty suit was waiting. I couldn't climb into the pantry and there were no hollow trees nearby.

I took hold of the wall. It felt easier to hold myself there than it had before. I gripped. I sidled, trembling, and I kept going, and tried very hard not to think as I held tight on to the outcrops that I was now above the hole. I didn't look behind me or down. I grabbed the extrusions and shuffled my poor feet like little animals into nooks and leaned on them to see if they'd take me, striving for the right pace, slow enough that I would not fall, quick enough that this would be over soon.

—

It was. I was there in the dark beyond the gap.

I pushed myself backward off the rock and landed in the rear part of the cave, the hollow beyond the pit, where I'd never been. I lay a long time gasping in the cold of the passage, trying to still my shaking limbs.

It was another country. I stared across at places I'd stood before. I was giddy and proud. I regarded the hole. I turned and went deeper into the hill, pausing to let my eyes adjust in shadows that were dense enough that I hallucinated, only a little, tiny points of light that weren't there.

I thought of kingdoms and crystal caves and the tunnel continued a few metres and the walls narrowed and I was in a shaft, a wedge which then closed up altogether so I had stone against my chest and my back and I tried a moment to press on, luxuriating in the terror of it, the sense that the hill had paused and would at any moment flex and offhandedly crush me.

So I stopped and pulled out of that embrace and sat with my back to the curving cold wall behind the hole, where my father couldn't touch me. I looked all the way out to where there was light. So deep in the hill even the waning light of the day glowed like a star. I waited.

He's here to count. There's a counting game, and I whispered its words as crows and magpies landed at the cave mouth, too effaced by light to be much as silhouettes, nothing more than ragged arrivals at the edge of darkness that I recognized by their calls. I sang a song you sing when you play a game of throwing stones. '*Up* the wall and *down* the well and *in* the boy and *out* the girl.'

I heard my father.

He called me. I put my hands over my mouth.

He was shouting. My heartbeat was hard enough to make me quake because there he was, a shadow at the entrance, only a little clearer than the fleeing birds. His legs were apart, his hands were up, braced on the top of the stone.

'You know what I hear?' he shouted. 'That there's a man here! Why's he not long gone with the other tallymen? Why'd you let him in? Know what I hear about this census-taker? This man you've let come? Know what I hear?'

He had not gone to the house, he had come straight to the hole, to me. How did he know where I would be, when even I hadn't? I held my mouth shut with my fingers.

'In town they told me there's a man who's come asking questions and they say he came here to speak to *you*. Where are you? What've you said to him? What's he doing here asking what isn't his business?'

It *was* his business. The man had said. My father stepped into the tunnel. He seemed to fill it, to block the light. 'Come on!' He shouted louder than I knew he could. 'Where are you? They were recalled! Why's this one still counting? This man thinks he knows what I've done? When? Always?'

I didn't speak or move. I was before him, against the rock, motionless in the dark shadow beyond the hole, a new place. He came to the edge of the rubbish pit and still he didn't see me there in front of him with my hands up.

'He's waiting to talk to me?' he shouted. 'Is that right? Is that what I hear?'

He turned at last. I watched his back. He was still calling when he walked away.

'I'll talk then,' he yelled to the hillside. 'You better come find me. You better come talk too. To me.'

I stayed quiet until I was certain he was beyond hearing then slumped and my held breath came out in a long whine. It was a long time until my trembling started to ebb at last and I could whisper another game song.

Very slowly the light in the cave mouth waned and I was more able to see the entrance itself, now that glow no longer effaced it. It was like an open eye, I thought – then I thought *No, it's like a closed eye*. Abruptly and precisely it was like the oval shape I see when I shut my eyes tight, the ebbing red glow like an opening leading into or out of something. I closed my eyes then but it was too dark to clearly see that vision that my body would conjure out of blood and the inside of skin when light hit it, but I'd seen it so often, examined it so carefully, that it wasn't hard for me to call to mind.

If I could squeeze my lids so tight that it almost brought me a headache – for long enough, in a bright enough place – the image would open with hazy edges like something living and particular and it would leave within its centre a smaller oval presence, floating.

I'd spent years making this appear in my inner eyes, and when I did so I would think myself in a cave looking out at a red sunset. Floating there in the cave mouth, I would imagine a boulder blocking all but the edge of my view.

I opened my eyes in a real cave, for a glimpse at the boulderless entrance beyond the split. It was filled with twilight. I closed my eyes again.

After a time I heard a scuffing, then laborious breaths.

—

'How did you get over there?'

It was the census-taker's voice. It was strained and not without admiration.

'I see you,' he said.

He hissed as he breathed. I heard his burdened steps.

'Now,' he said. He spoke in little bursts. 'Don't,' he said, 'open,' he said, 'your eyes.'

He didn't stagger. He trod slowly and deliberately and with care. 'Keep your eyes closed,' he said. 'What do you see?'

'The entrance to a tunnel,' I said without hesitation. 'Like this one but red.'

'What else?'

'A rock floating in the middle.' This wasn't true: I couldn't see that now, only vague dark forms. If I'd been older and seen more things in the world they might have put me in mind of fleeting deep-sea things.

'Tell me about the rock,' he said. He hefted something. I heard a burden fall to the ground. 'Now look carefully inside your eyes and tell me what you see there. Don't look here. Do you promise me?'

'It's like an egg.' I considered what I'd see floating in the cave mouth behind my eyes. 'It's the shape of an egg . . .'

'You promise?'

'I promise.'

He grunted in satisfaction and exhaled and I heard the scrape of a mass pushed forward.

'Tell me,' he said, 'what you *want* to see.'

That caught me up short. I had nothing to say. Which meant there was a silence during which I could hear him shoving.

'Anything,' he prompted.

'I don't know,' I said. 'Maybe – anything?'

'Anything!' he said. 'Wait now,' he said. 'Eyes very closed. Quiet now one second.'

He hissed and I heard stones pattering and the sharp ricochets as they bounced below me and then a scraping roll and several hard diminishing thumps and a crack below as something heavy fell.

The last of it was replaced by silence.

I kept my eyes closed. I heard the man softly clap his hands. I heard his feet on the tunnel floor.

'All right,' he said. 'Look at me.'

I opened my eyes.

He stood on the edge of the pit. He held his hands out above it, opening and closing his fingers to rid them of dirt.

He looked at me, perhaps kindly. Patiently.

'How did you get over there?' he said. 'Can you get back?'

I went to the cave wall. I didn't want to hesitate in front of him. I set out to cross it again by those handholds.

The man reached out and plucked me from the wall when I was only halfway done. He made me gasp as he braced himself and snatched me. It was so quick, and there I was, blinking foolishly on his side of things, back where I'd always been before.

He put his hand on my shoulder.

'There,' he said.

There were many things I wanted to say, to ask him, but I couldn't yet speak.

—

It was fully night. I looked past him at the dark side of the hill and the foliage and stone in the sundown. I heard another whinnying honk.

'Your mule,' I said quickly, so he'd know I was just startled, not afraid.

He gestured down the hill and pursed his lips and before he spoke I said, 'There's no one in town for me,' and it was he who was startled this time. He looked at me with interest and care.

'I had . . .' I said, and thought of Samma and of Drobe and didn't know how to explain them. On the bridge, Samma might soon hook for bats, at least. 'One can't do any more for me and one's gone,' I said. 'Drobe's his name.'

That made the man look away from me, down the dark slopes. He seemed to hold his breath.

At which, though I'd been about to tell him more, I stopped. Wherever he was now I had no more to say about poor Drobe.

'There's no one,' I said in the end.

The man nodded and released his breath and walked out of the cave and waited where the hill began.

'Do you have food in your house?' he said.

'You can't come in.'

'I *know*. You're good at rules. That's good. I was thinking of you, for the food. Do you have something?'

'Yes.'

'And you could . . .' he said, and got lost in thought.

'So,' he said eventually, hurriedly. 'Like I said, sometimes there are *tasks arising* – any jobs that the numbers tell me need doing. It's my job to do them. We had trouble where I come from. Fighting. What we realized is that the more you know about your people, the better. That's why I go counting.

'I had someone who worked for me.' He spoke carefully. 'But she listened to tattle. About me. And in the end she took off with records and messages that weren't hers to take. She's gone now. Papers re-filed.

'I need a replacement.

'They told me about your father and mother and they told me about you. Law goes through the blood a bit. I'll mark you in my books whatever happens, which makes you my business, and makes the books your business too. You could learn them.'

He stopped. I willed him to continue.

'I need an intern,' he said. 'Would you like to come with me?'

I said, 'Yes.'

The man walked down the hill by a route I'd never have taken. I followed him to a crag. He showed me the lights of the town and the darkness of the other hill beyond them and the gorge yawning below, and the bridge. There was a glow of neon, somewhere with places open late. A district on the other side that I didn't recognize from where we were, that was like somewhere I'd never seen, somewhere just opened.

'I could teach you,' he said. 'To do what I do.'

'An apprentice,' I said.

'No. A trainee. I'll train you. We'll be *colleagues*.' I'd come to understand that word. 'If you come to work with me we'll be in the same department. I'll be your line manager.'

'Where's yours?'

He frowned. 'A long way away back home.'

'What'll happen?' I said.

At first he didn't answer. We walked back to my house. Then he said, 'Hey,' when it came into view, so I quickly turned to listen.

He said, 'Will you give me your attention? If you work with me you might hear difficult things but I need you to stay focused. Think you can do that? And it might be scary sometimes. Can you be brave?

'There's – an *agent* – of something – who's been trailing

me a long time.' He shook his head. 'Trying to catch me up, saying things. It can trick you. Issuing good forgeries, using the right language. I have to keep ahead of it. If someone told you stories about me, would you believe them?'

I shook my head when I understood that was what he required.

'I *do* have this authority. To make this count. So will you.'

He smiled and stilled my new unease. I was eager to make this count, as he said.

'Bring what you want,' he said, pointing me into the house. 'What you can.'

One more looking through the windows. Two shirts. What books I could find. Samma's little knife, which I stared at, which I'd forgotten. I went through every room. Some oatcakes. Two pencils.

In my father's workroom I looked at the table all mucky with metal dust. The room felt saturated with his presence, felt like he was speaking in it.

I didn't take any of his keys.

Tucked behind his worktable was the message in looped blue ink that was or was not my mother's. I blinked to see it there. That I took.

In the upstairs room I used the knife to score around the edges of the image I'd drawn on the wallpaper. I teased with the point and tried to lift my animals off the wall to carry them with me. But the glue was too strong and the paper came off in strips and they tore away.

I took the house key from the hook in the kitchen. It should have been dark when I came out but it was as if there was grey light under the hill's stones.

The man fetched his mule. It met my eyes in challenge.

'What do you have?' he said. I started to justify everything I carried but he just opened a pannier for me to put it in.

'My goat!' I said. I ran to it and it hawed and hustled me.

'You should bring it,' the man said, giving it a wave of welcome.

'You took the other one,' I said.

He frowned. He shook his head.

'I wouldn't steal,' he said.

'Who took it, then?' I said.

'There's no shortage of thieves.'

'I thought you took it. I thought I heard you shoot.'

'You might have done. But,' he said then, 'not your goat.'

I closed the door of my house. I locked it. 'You came here because I was here, didn't you?' I said. I looked at the key I held.

'Wait,' I said.

I ran to where I'd buried the bottle. It was too heavy to bring. I couldn't let those remains moulder without me. I couldn't bring myself to smash that thick glass even had I the strength. I pulled it out of the earth and shook it and the bones rattled.

You could put a bird's egg in there and let it grow in the glass. Drobe hadn't said if anyone had ever put a baby in a bottle and let it continue. You could. Push food in, teach it through the glass, clean it out. If you were strong enough. You could grow a man in there, a woman, in the glass.

I didn't smash the bottle but I did at last upend it and scatter the bones.

I put my house key into the bottle and stopped it up again and nestled it carefully in a hollow of dried weeds and stone, where the bones it had contained could watch it.

He said, 'Let's put this place out of our sight.'

Halfway between what had been my house and the bridgetown the man clicked within his throat and veered off the path.

I was so surprised I stopped at the edge of the rough and watched him. He turned to face me and walked backward to keep up with his mule. He beckoned as he went so I stepped after him among the stones, pulling my goat. It came, complaining.

'Careful,' the man said. 'We're going wherever there are people to count.' The mule sniffed but I thought it sounded happy.

The coming darkness and the picking of the plantlife against my ragged trousers and the sway of our step-by-step descent narcotized me so I felt myself retreat behind my eyes, watching from a long way back, listening to my own body until after some hours at the start of deep night as we approached a spreading canopy, the foothills and the hill's forested surrounds, the census-taker woke me for a startled moment by lifting me to put me in the saddle, nestled between bags. I fell asleep again, proper asleep, at once.

Much later I lurched half out of a bad dream with a cry, shaking, my hands clutching for something. Perhaps the animals had sounded. I don't think so.

We were in the wooded lowland, I realized. We were off the hill.

I looked still sleepily at the flat land that somehow did not shock me alert, or all the way awake.

This Is My Catechism, it says in my second book, a book started, confiscated, pilfered, regained, and that I've inherited, that my boss taught me slowly to read, the few scraps left of which I go over many times, and ultimately in which now I write.

And there'd come to be a lot to write, a diaspora of which to make sense. An aftermath of war and commerce. Numbers to run, in as many kinds of places as there are places, cities you could call invisible or uneasy or beleaguered, cities about which I won't even start to write here, in this part of my second book that can only be a prologue. There would be functions to apply according to instructions, which I can do without insubordination.

My line manager rarely speaks about my predecessor.

It wasn't my catechism that fronts this, to which I've at last responded with my five words on two lines, and with all of this; it was hers, the message she needed to give me, to give whoever came after her. It is mine now, though. Written with her unorthodox precision and inserted at the start of what would become my second book too, I've keyed it many times with the muffled typewriter, with its hacking bird sound: I write it again now, in full, by hand.

The Hope Is So:
Count Entire Nation. Subsume Under Sets. -
Take Accounts. Keep Estimates. Realize
Interests. So
Reach Our Government's Ultimate Ends.

‘I dreamed of the hole,’ I murmured. I rolled with the mule. I heard the man and his voice calmed me. He was close and I was unafraid.

I dreamed of the hole, I said. I remember saying it, but I don’t remember the dream exactly, though all my memories before that moment and after – forever after, you might say – had and have to them a must and coldness that can only have come from inside a hill. I’ve supposed that these recollections are what make me fretful at introspective times, so I believe what I said was true, but too, I think I dreamed of another city than that conical one of the discarded, that I’d visited that place I’d started to draw between the flowers on the wall, the uncertain charcoal city bustling with citizens of endless kinds and business, the limits of which spread out so every country I would ultimately come to, in which to count those I’d learn are my scattered compatriots and my business, would be in its outskirts, and I according to some purpose looking for the message left for me there, and counting there too.

There were rises in the distance, against the clouded sky behind us. I counted absences in my head. One of the rises must have been the hill, with its counter-hill, and its bridge, from where I’d come, from which my manager and I were just newly descended.